Melanie's To-Do List

1. *Buy the perfect house.*

2. *Make appointment with sperm bank at perfect time of the month.*

3. *Paint nursery the perfect baby-duck yellow.*

4. *Bring newest neighbour perfect housewarming gift.*

5. *Admire new neighbour's perfect rear view.*

6. *Flee in horror. New neighbour is perfectly disastrous ex-husband!*

7. *DO NOT GIVE IN TO DANGEROUS ATTRACTION!*

8. *Give in to dangerous attraction.*

9. *Panic!*

Dear Reader,

Welcome to the breathtaking world of Silhouette Sensation.

Men are born to be heroes in our FIRST-BORN SONS mini-series which continues this month with Ruth Wind's *Born Brave*. Look out for another instalment next month.

Ever-popular author Ruth Langan starts her brand-new trilogy THE LASSITER LAW where *By Honour Bound* gets us off to a cracking start. Don't forget the following book's out next month.

Kylie Brant brings us the irresistible and thrilling conclusion to her CHARMED AND DANGEROUS trilogy with *Hard To Tame*. We also have a reunion story with a twist in Carla Cassidy's *Once Forbidden…*, which is part of THE DELANEY HEIRS series, a secretive protector with a heart of gold in Judith Duncan's *The Renegade and the Heiress* and a drop-dead-gorgeous cop in Mary McBride's *Baby, Baby, Baby*.

Happy Halloween!

The Editors

Baby, Baby, Baby

MARY McBRIDE

™ SILHOUETTE®
SENSATION™

*First published in Great Britain 2002
Silhouette Books, Eton House, 18-24 Paradise Road,
Richmond, Surrey TW9 1SR*

© Mary Myers 2001

ISBN 0 373 27191 3

18-1002

*Printed and bound in Spain
by Litografia Rosés S.A., Barcelona*

MARY McBRIDE

When it comes to writing romance, historical or contempory, Mary McBride is a natural. What else would anyone expect from someone whose parents met on a blind date on Valentine's Day, and who met her own husband—whose middle name just happens to be Valentine—on February 14, as well?

She lives in St. Louis, Missouri, with her husband and two sons. Mary loves to hear from readers. You can write to her c/o PO Box 411202, St. Louis, MO 63141, USA or contact her online at McBride101@aol.com

For Pete and Mary Pancella,
who make such lovely music together

Chapter 1

Melanie Sears couldn't help but grin. Not only was it her last day at work, but her boss, the mayor, an elegant if not arrogant man who was addicted to hundred-dollar haircuts and thousand-dollar suits, was down on his pin-striped Armani knees, begging her to stay.

"I'll be back in eighteen months, Sam."

"Things are falling apart already." While he whined, His Honor gestured through his office door toward the reception area. "Look how badly your surprise party turned out."

Melanie didn't disagree, but then, even with her own amazing organizational skills, she would have been hard-pressed to bring off the perfect celebratory combination of congratulations on a job well done, happy semi-retirement and baby shower. She knew for a fact, however, that if she had been in charge of her own party, the paper plates and napkins wouldn't have said Bon Voyage, that she wouldn't in a million years have served a punch whose main ingredient was Tang, and that she would never, *ever,* even at gunpoint, have hired a mime.

"What the devil was in that punch?" Mayor Venneman stood and began to pick carpet lint from his trousers. "Motor oil?"

She told him about the powdered orange drink and then laughed as she watched his pinstripes shiver. "I'm sure it won't happen again with Cleo in charge. I gave her a list of preferred caterers, but maybe I should make another copy, just in case."

"Maybe you should stay." He slumped into the big leather chair behind his desk, looking more like a petulant two-year-old than the savvy and suave politician he was. "Why do you need to take eighteen months off to have a baby? Why can't you do what everybody else does? Work until the bitter end, then come back thin and frazzled after a three-month maternity leave with all those nasty pumps and jars and pictures of the kid? Why do you want to have a baby anyway?"

"Actually I want two," Melanie said with a laugh. "You're going to have to go through this again in a few more years, Sam. Better get used to it. I've got it all planned out."

Planning was what Melanie did best. When she was ten years old, her mother died, entrusting her only daughter with the care and feeding of Dr. Henry Von

Briggle Sears, Ph.D., poet, painter, and perfect specimen of the absentminded professor. Far from considering it a burden, Melanie thrived on making lists, scheduling appointments and seeing they were kept, even making sure that Pop turned in grades to the art history department on time each semester.

While most young girls were learning makeup tricks and fantasizing about their teen idols, Melanie was learning how to balance a checkbook and pay bills and compile lists of dependable plumbers and repairmen. Instead of developing a fondness for lipstick and costume jewelry, she grew enamored of calendars with large spaces, Rolodexes, and Post-It notes.

They'd lived in a huge, century-old, redbrick monstrosity just a few blocks from the university. Pop's studio on the third floor was the only room where a person had to pick his way through a maze of easels and battered boxes and waist-high piles of books, where every chair was occupied whether or not someone was sitting in it, where the slightest movement might send canvasses toppling like dominoes or set off an explosion of dust motes in the air. The rest of the house was dustless and serene, thanks to Melanie, with a place for everything and everything in its proper place. Always.

"Life isn't solely about order," her father had told her more than once. But Melanie wasn't so sure.

Not back then. Not now, either.

"Lighten up," people told her.

But the one time in her thirty-one years that she'd

lightened up and let go of her beloved lists had been a disaster. Love or lust, or whatever it was she felt for Sonny Randle the minute she'd laid eyes on him two years ago, had rendered her temporarily insane. She must've been certifiably nuts to marry him after knowing him only a few weeks. But since the divorce a year ago she was sane again, and fiercely determined to stay that way.

After Melanie left Sam Venneman whining and wringing his manicured hands in his office, she took one last look through the drawers of her desk and behind the sliding doors of her credenza in the unlikely chance that she'd overlooked something earlier in the week. The drawers were empty. Not even a lone paper clip remained. It was the same for the credenza. All the cupboards were bare.

Stashed unobtrusively in a corner were the belongings of her replacement, Cleo Pierce. The former anchorwoman for the local NBC affiliate hadn't had to be asked twice to shelve her consulting business to take on a job that would put her in constant contact with Sam Venneman, America's Most Eligible Mayor. Not only had Cleo eagerly signed on as the interim executive assistant, but she'd insisted on a contract that clearly specified that the position would be hers for the entire eighteen months of Melanie's planned leave of absence.

There was no going back now, but then, Melanie had no intention of changing her mind. It was, after all, a perfect plan.

Her other position at city hall, that of director of

community relations, had been more difficult to fill on a temporary basis. In fact, Sam was still interviewing candidates. The pay wasn't all that great, hardly enough to buy aspirin for all the headaches involved when trying to please nearly two hundred neighborhood associations, each with its own agenda. Some of them needed tax abatements to entice new residents; many needed grants to fix up deteriorating playgrounds and parks; all of them, including her own Channing Square Residents Association, were pleading for higher police visibility and more foot patrols.

To that end, a little over a year ago Melanie had come up with the Cop on the Block program, which would guarantee low-cost loans to officers who agreed to live in selected high-crime areas of the city. The program was her pet project, her baby, and after she'd steamrolled it through the board of aldermen, she'd schmoozed and cajoled and nearly arm-wrestled half the bankers in town until a few of them agreed to provide the loans in return for the unbounded gratitude of city hall and unlimited luncheon invitations and photo opportunities with Sam Venneman and any national dignitaries who visited him.

Although Melanie hadn't seen the actual paperwork, the first Cop on the Block loan had been approved just this week, so that had been part of the celebration at her surprise party this afternoon in addition to her leave of absence and imminent motherhood.

Speaking of which, she told herself, she should probably get out of here before one more person asked when the baby was due and then stood counting fingers and looking perplexed when she answered early next January, a full nine months away, or before Claude Davis of the parks department came up with another joke about sperm banks.

Melanie took one last glance around her office. It looked so aimless without her planner open on the desk and so bleak without her collection of Pop's watercolors on the walls. There were only rectangular outlines now to show where they had hung. She hoped Cleo wouldn't paint the walls some horrible shade of green or make any permanent changes that would surely drive her crazy when she returned next September.

Most of all, she hoped things didn't go completely to hell in a handbasket the minute she left city hall.

Well, maybe just a little.

It was nice to be appreciated.

On the way to her car, as always, Melanie slowed her pace to admire the flower beds that surrounded city hall. Since it was April, the grounds were awash in tulips—stately red ones, so perfect they almost looked fake, and smaller yellow ones with waxy leaves and frilly petals. In a few months they'd be replaced by a profusion of daisies and purple salvia. Come autumn, the old limestone building would look gorgeous as it rose from beds of bronze chrysanthemums. Claude Davis of the parks department might have told lousy jokes about sperm banks, but he was a hell of a planner when it came to gardens. Maybe she'd call him next week to give her some ideas for the little space she wanted to plant in her backyard now that she'd have ample time to tend it.

She was pulling her little planner from her handbag to make a note to herself about Claude when she heard the clack of high heels on the sidewalk just behind her and turned to see Peg Harrel, the mayor's longtime secretary, rushing to catch up.

"Are you really sure this is what you want to do, Melanie?" Peg bent her platinum-colored, pixie-haircut head to light what was probably the first cigarette she'd had since her lunch break at noon. "Single parenthood isn't any bed of roses, you know. It's a bummer, actually. My kids would be the first to tell you."

"I'm really, really sure, Peg." If she'd said it once, she'd said it a million times lately. Maybe she shouldn't have been so honest and forthcoming about her plan to get pregnant, but she was so thrilled about this baby and had wanted to share the news with everyone at city hall if not the entire city.

Melanie closed her planner with a little thump and continued in the direction of the parking lot with Peg smoking up a storm at her side. "The party was fun, Peg. Thanks for putting it together. I never suspected a thing."

"I'll bet you did."

"No. Not for a second. Honest," Melanie lied.

"What did you think of the mime?" The woman nudged her arm. "Wasn't he a riot?"

Melanie nodded politely although she thought cloying would have been a better description. She wondered vaguely if the world was divided into people who enjoyed mimes and people who ran the other way—screaming—when they saw one coming.

A few yards from her spiffy little yellow Miata, soon to be traded in on a sensible minivan, Melanie reached into her bag for her keys and then sighed. "Leaving isn't going to be quite as easy at I thought it would be. I'll really miss everybody. Plus, I'm not used to not working."

"Oh, you'll be working, kiddo." Peg laughed and rolled her eyes. "Trust me. You'll be working. You just won't be getting paid for it."

"Well, that's true, I guess."

"You'll be working twenty times harder than you ever did here. So, when's the big day?"

"Monday. My appointment is at eleven, so by noon I ought to be one slightly and happily pregnant lady."

"No kidding. Does it always work the first time?"

"It will with me," Melanie said, her voice infused with every bit of the confidence she felt. Even though her OB-GYN had cautioned her that three, sometimes four artificial inseminations were the norm before a pregnancy "took," she was positive that Monday would be her day and that her baby's birthday would be in the first week of January. It was just too perfectly planned to go wrong.

Peg wrapped her cigarette-free arm around Melanie's shoulders and gave her a hug. "Well, good luck, kiddo. We'll try to hold it together while you're gone. Keep us posted."

"I will. Thanks again, Peg."

The woman started to walk away, then stopped. "Oh, with all of the excitement of the party, I almost forgot to tell you. You know that cop who was shot last week? The one who got blown through the plate-glass window?"

"What about him?" As she asked, she could feel that tiny fault line in her heart begin to quiver the way it always did whenever she heard the words "cop" and "shot" in the same sentence.

In this particular case, the officer had been hit during a raid on a crack house in the Bienville neighborhood, one of the highest crime areas in the city. He'd been wearing a bulletproof vest, thank God, but the direct hit had still managed to propel him backward ten or fifteen feet, through a window and out onto the sidewalk. His name was still being withheld from the press, and Melanie had found the whole incident so disturbing that she'd avoided all the memos that referenced it. Even now, having asked, "What about him?" she really didn't want to know.

"Guess who it was?" Peg asked.

From the way the woman's eyebrows climbed halfway up her forehead and her mouth kind of oozed to the side, Melanie didn't have to guess. But before she could prevent the answer she didn't want to hear, Peg exclaimed, "Your ex!"

"Oh." While the fault line inside her slipped another tiny notch, she struggled to come up with some sort of appropriate comment. "Well, I'm glad he wasn't hurt."

"Me, too. Sonny hasn't stopped by city hall in quite a while now, has he? Two or three months at least."

Melanie nodded. It had been two months and two weeks, to be exact, and she didn't even have to consult her calendar to remember. Her ex-husband's entrances and exits were always indelible.

"Maybe he finally knows the meaning of the word divorce," Melanie said. She could have said maybe he'd finally taken her threat of a restraining order seriously. And somewhere in a far corner of her heart she wondered if it was because he didn't care anymore.

Peg sighed a little cloud of cigarette smoke. "I always enjoyed seeing him, even if you didn't. I used to keep lollipops in my desk for him when he was trying to quit smoking. Red ones."

"I remember." She also remembered how those damned red lollipops increased the sensuality of Sonny's already way-too-sexy mouth and how many times she'd wanted to kiss him, just to see if he still tasted as good as he looked.

All of a sudden she noticed that Peg was standing there silent and staring at her as if waiting for a reply to a question Melanie hadn't even heard.

"I'm sorry. Did you say something?"

"Just that it's a shame to be having artificial insemination when the genuine article is…"

"I'd better get going, Peg, before the traffic gets too bad." Melanie stabbed her key in the car lock, opened the door, and tossed her handbag inside.

''Thanks again for the wonderful party. Hold down the fort while I'm gone, huh? And don't let Cleo do anything too bizarre to my office, okay?''

''Oh, sure. Good luck, Melanie. But I still think...''

'''Bye, Peg.''

The genuine article.

Peg's words kept sneaking into Melanie's thoughts no matter how she tried to dismiss them. It was a good thing she could have made the drive from city hall to Channing Square with her eyes closed because images of Sonny kept distracting her from the worse-than-usual Friday rush-hour traffic inching south on Grant Parkway.

The genuine article.

The first time she'd ever seen him, Solomon Stephen ''Sonny'' Randle had looked like a genuine bum and smelled as if he'd just climbed out of a Dumpster.

Two years ago, during one of Mayor Venneman's forays to New York to do the morning talk shows, Melanie had presided in his absence at an awards ceremony for the police department. Always a nervous wreck at such occasions, she'd been even worse that afternoon, sitting up front with the chief of police and various dignitaries, trying to keep her trembling knees together in the way-too-short skirt of her gray gabardine suit.

After she'd made an equally short, rather gray-gabardine speech, she had handed out a score of letters of commendation to fresh-faced young patrolmen in dress blue uniforms with gleaming buttons, and presented half a dozen certificates of valor to older, but no less natty, officers. Then she called the name on the final certificate—Lieutenant Solomon S. Randle—and watched in horror as a bearded derelict shambled from the back of the auditorium to the podium where she stood.

Only the fact that the audience had cheered wildly—including the brass behind her on the stage— kept Melanie from screaming "Somebody stop him!" She'd presented the certificate with one hand while using the other to discretely wave away the garbage stench emanating from the awardee.

Afterward, at the reception that followed, he had come up to her like an ill wind, but one carrying two glasses of champagne.

"Here. Hold these a second," he'd said in a voice that ranged somewhere between rough gravel and harsh cigarette smoke.

Melanie held the wet glasses, then watched in awe as the derelict cop proceeded to divest himself of one greasy beard, two straggly eyebrows, a terrible scar, and several gold front teeth, to emerge—Oh, Lord, had he emerged!—as the most gorgeous man Melanie had ever seen in her life.

He'd still smelled to high heaven in his undercover garments, but by then she almost hadn't cared.

The three weeks that followed had been not just a whirlwind, but a complete sensual blur unlike anything she had ever experienced until she'd woken up married in Sonny's disheveled downtown loft.

She now woke up at the wheel of her Miata on

Grant Parkway to realize she had missed her turn onto Channing Avenue. Melanie cursed her ex-husband for derailing her again, then circled around in the terrible traffic and finally made the turn onto Channing only to find herself behind a moving van that seemed intent on going three miles per hour and hitting its brakes every few hundred feet.

Anyplace else and she might have given the truck an irritated beep of her horn to speed it up, but since it appeared that somebody was moving in, Melanie was patient. Heaven knows Channing Square needed all the residents it could get. Besides, she didn't mind driving slowly because it gave her a chance to look around and to savor the late-afternoon spring in Channing Park, one of the oldest and most beautiful in the city.

Although she'd only lived here a year, as the recording secretary and official historian for the Channing Square Residents Association, Melanie knew this little corner of the city inside out. The park's thirty acres had been dedicated in 1845, but the grand residences that surrounded it hadn't started going up until after the Civil War. In the 1870s they had risen with a Victorian vengeance, one graceful Second Empire town house after another, and then the staunch redbrick Federals and the somber Romanesque Revivals. For a few glorious decades Channing Square had been the most prestigious address in the city.

Then, as happened in so many cities, the rich folks had moved on to bigger and better homes, leaving the

mansions in Channing Square behind to suffer the
consequences of the coming years. And suffer they
did, especially during the Depression when most had
been cut up into small apartments. By the 1980s the
once-great neighborhood had become a slum with
half of its homes' windows boarded up and crack
dealers holding sway on every corner. The beautiful
park had been overgrown with trash trees and weeds,
its lovely Victorian bandstand, which had once played
host to the John Philip Sousa Band, becoming a place
to turn quick tricks or to stash dead bodies in the dark
of the night.

All of that changed in the mid-eighties when a few
brave souls moved back from the suburbs. A few
more followed, and a few more, until finally the rec-
lamation was in full swing. At last count, a hundred
twenty of the square's two hundred houses were occupied and undergoing some form of rehab, all the
way from the early, gritty stages of demolition to the
delicate finishing touches of paint on the cornices.

Melanie had loved every minute of the year she'd
lived here. Her own Victorian painted lady was on
Kassing Avenue, just to the west of the park. After
she'd moved out of Sonny's loft, she'd bought the
small limestone-fronted Second Empire town house
from Dieter Weist, the architect who was rehabbing
it on spec. He'd finished the first floor and two second-floor bedrooms for her in record time. All that
remained to be done now was the nursery and the
playroom that would take up the entire third floor.
During the next nine months that was what she

planned to do so everything would be ready for the arrival of little Alex or Alexis in January.

There were far worse places to raise a child, she'd decided. Channing Square was a neighborhood in every sense of the word. It was like a small town where the residents all knew one another, worked together, and looked out for their neighbors' safety and well-being. If the crime rate hadn't come down quite as far as she would have preferred, that problem ought to be remedied somewhat in the future by the Cop on the Block program.

When the moving van turned onto Kassing, Melanie smiled and made a little thumbs-up sign. All right! Now if it just stopped at the rattrap of a house next door to hers, the house everyone feared was destined to be the last to ever be renovated, her day would be complete. No, her next several years would be complete without the constant worry of living next door to an abandoned Victorian nightmare.

The van's brake lights flared once more just before the driver signaled he was pulling over to park in front of the big red brick place at 1224 Kassing Avenue. Melanie waved cheerfully as she passed by to turn into her driveway at 1222.

Life was good. It was very, very good. Come Monday, it would be just about perfect.

The tradition in Channing Square was to welcome new residents as soon as possible with a small gift, usually something edible and preferably homemade. Being the soul of organization that she was, Melanie kept a stash of her buttermilk blueberry muffins in the freezer for just such an occasion, so she picked out half a dozen, tied quick blue ribbons on each one, and arranged them in a wicker basket with a blue-and-white checked napkin.

"Eat your heart out, Martha Stewart," she thought as she trotted down her front steps, then followed two men and a king-size mattress up the steps and through the front door of 1224.

What a mess! With some of the windows still boarded, it was dark inside but still light enough to see that the place was a shambles. In what had once been a grand front parlor to her right, she couldn't tell the pattern on the ancient wallpaper for all the dirt and water stains. A great hole gaped in the wall where a marble fireplace had once been. There was mold growing across the ceiling and trash—a Dumpster's worth—all over the floor.

Her new neighbors certainly had their work cut out for them. Up until that moment her excitement had pretty much been confined to the sale of the property alone. But now Melanie actually started thinking about the neighbors themselves. She wondered if they had children. Her perfect world might become even more so if one or two potential baby-sitters moved in right next door, or even better, future playmates. A smile crossed her lips as she imagined a little girl calling, "Mom, I'm going next door to play with Alexis" or a little boy yelling across the yard, "Hey, Alex. Wanna ride bikes?"

She glanced around in the hope of seeing the peo-

ple who would undoubtedly come to play such a huge
role in her life. She'd feed their children peanut butter
and jelly sandwiches with carrot sticks. Maybe she'd
sit with them in little chairs at the kindergarten Christmas program. Maybe her daughter would marry the
boy next door. All of a sudden, instead of welcoming
new neighbors, she felt as if she were about to greet
her future.

"Excuse me, lady," somebody said behind her.
Melanie stepped aside to let two men and a big-screen
TV pass by.

"Is the owner around?" she asked.

"I think he's in the kitchen," one of the men said.

Assuming the kitchen was at the back of the house,
Melanie picked her way carefully down the dark, gar-
bage-strewn hallway. Her nose identified dust and
mold along with countless other odors she didn't even
want to name. What a rattrap. If something small and
furry skittered across one of her feet, she was going
to toss her welcoming basket of goodies in the general
direction of the kitchen and make a beeline for the
front door.

If she'd had any sense she would have changed into
her sneakers rather than wear the new pair of black
Ferragamo pumps she'd worn to work that day. The
soles kept sticking to the floor as she walked, and she
could only hope it was bubble gum that she'd have
to be cleaning off later. A little shiver of ickiness ran
down her spine.

"Hello?" she called out. "Anybody home?"

When no one answered, Melanie decided she'd

leave her welcome basket with a note saying she'd
drop by tomorrow. She stepped through a doorway
into a kitchen that was quite a bit brighter than the
rest of the house and not nearly as trashed. There was
a man standing at the sink, drinking from the plastic
top of a thermos. His back was to her so all she could
see was longish hair, a pair of wide shoulders, and
the lovely hug of faded denim over one truly great
male butt.

How come whenever she hired moving men they
always turned out to be thugs with crew cuts and beer
bellies rather than pure hunks like this guy? She was
making a mental note to get the name and number of
the moving company from the side of the van when
the hunk at the sink slowly turned around.

Melanie made a little strangling sound deep in her
throat, then gasped, "Oh, my God!"

He cocked his head, setting that killer grin of his
on a sexy, almost perilous slant. "Hello, darlin'."

"What the hell do you think you're doing here,
Sonny?"

"I live here, Mel. I'm the new Cop on the Block."
His gorgeous blue-one-minute, green-the-next gaze
strayed to the basket of muffins in her hands. "Are
those for me?"

Chapter 2

It was a good thing Sonny Randle had quick reflexes, otherwise he'd have a shiner the size of Oregon thanks to the rocklike frozen muffin his ex-wife had hurled at him just before she'd turned and fled the kitchen.

He ignored the slight tremor in his hand as he refilled the red plastic cap of his thermos and stood at the sink sipping his lukewarm coffee and watching Mel storm across her driveway and back into her house. A moment later, one by one, he watched the interior shutters on the south side of the house snap closed.

Okay. No surprise there. It was exactly what he'd expected. The muffin had been unanticipated, however. Actually, he was probably lucky that she'd thrown a muffin at him instead of a brick.

Suddenly one of her shutters opened a fraction, just enough for Sonny to discern her silhouette as she peeked out. He couldn't see her face, but he knew her eyes were giving off hot blue sparks and she was grinding her teeth and clenching her fists, already making a mental list—complete with Roman numerals and subheadings—of what she was going to do to get rid of the menace next door.

He smiled and lifted his hand in a friendly little wave, then watched the shutter snap closed again.

You can run, babe, and you can hide, but it's not going to do you any damned good. Now that I know what I did wrong, I know how to do this right. And we're so right, Mel. You and I.

"Hey, Lieutenant," a voice called from the hallway. "Where do you want this couch?"

"Be right there."

Sonny drained the last of his coffee and screwed the cap back on the thermos without taking his eyes off the battened-down house next door. Right about now Melanie would be wound in a tight little ball in the corner of her own couch, her long legs tucked beneath her and her soft, shiny hair hooked firmly behind her ears and her lower lip wedged between her teeth while she took pen in hand to compose her battle plan.

The siege had officially begun.

Number One on her list was calling city hall, but that proved to be useless on a Friday at almost six o'clock when everyone had gone home. Melanie swore as she slammed the receiver back into its cradle, then looked at her list again because she was so upset she'd forgotten what Number Two was.

Right. Call Mike Kaczinski, Sonny's partner, to see just what the hell her ex-husband was up to. She didn't believe for one millisecond that he had taken out a loan, low-cost or otherwise, to buy the place next door. Cop on the Block, her aunt Fanny's sweet behind! Lieutenant Sonny Randle not only *worked* undercover vice, he also ate, slept, and breathed it. What did he want a house for? He was never home!

Melanie stalked to the window again and opened the shutter a quarter of an inch. Squinting fiercely, she could see the movers close the back of their truck as they prepared to leave. There was no evidence of the new alleged homeowner. She craned her neck and angled her head so she could look down his driveway where his horrible muscle car sat like a black pit bull chained to a cement block. Wonderful. If he really was moving in, she had that roaring engine to look forward to at all hours of the night.

It was starting to get dark so she closed the shutter tightly and turned on a lamp in the living room. The exposed brick of the walls was always warm and comforting, and seemed no less so now that she was about to have a nervous breakdown. She went back to her cozy corner of the couch, pulled up her feet, and hugged her arms around herself, pretending for a moment that this wasn't happening, that the perfection she'd experienced just half an hour ago was still possible.

She gazed around at the lovely haven she'd created for herself here in this more-than-a-century-old house in its antiquated cranny of the city. Almost all of the furniture had belonged to her parents so, just like them, it was an odd blend of elegant and eccentric. The camel-back Victorian sofa was upholstered in a rich rose silk and piled with bright needlepoint pillows that her father had designed. Just to her right, on the marble-topped table beside the sofa was the bronze-and-stained-glass lamp Pop had made, with its shade like lovely bits of melted rubies and emeralds and sapphires. Scattered across the floor were the Persian rugs her mother had collected.

On the other side of the foyer, the dining room was an odd but somehow perfect blend of American and European antiques. Beyond that, the kitchen was a cozy mix of blue-and-white Portuguese tiles and gleaming copper and brass.

While the whole house was colorful and eccentric, it was also neat and orderly, just the way Melanie liked it. The way she needed it. There was security in order, in having everything in its proper place. She wasn't fussy, though. And she certainly wasn't Felix Unger, although that's who she'd felt like when she shared Sonny's Oscar-Madison-like space.

Sonny.

Damn.

Casting a baleful glance at the list she'd left by the phone, she realized she couldn't call Mike Kaczinski. Not at the Third Precinct, anyway. If he had been involved in last Friday's shooting, along with Sonny, then he'd probably be on leave or vacation, too. That also meant that the new Cop on the damned Block would have time on his hands and nothing to do but aggravate her until he went back to work.

Fine. Let him try. She'd keep her shutters closed and her doors locked and she wouldn't answer the phone. There was plenty of food in the fridge and freezer. She didn't have to go out. At least not until…

Oh, my God. Her appointment Monday at eleven.

No. Don't even think about that right now, she warned herself. *Don't think about the little vial packed in dry ice that arrived just yesterday at Dr. Wentworth's office from the sperm bank in Chicago. How long did those little guys last?* She couldn't remember.

If she cancelled and set a new appointment for next month, that would shift everything. Everything! Instead of being born in January, her baby wouldn't be born until February. Then, instead of being a determined and hardworking Capricorn, Little Alex or Alexis would be a quirky Aquarius. Oh, Lord. Instead of having a little photocopy of herself, she'd be giving birth to a Sonny.

She was shuddering at the very thought when her doorbell suddenly chimed.

Don't answer it. Let him stand out there all night, all weekend, all year.

But being the orderly soul that she was, Melanie couldn't stand not responding to a ringing phone or the repeated ding-dongs coming from her front door. She opened it a crack, then let out a tiny bleat of relief

when she saw that it wasn't Sonny, but rather Joan
Carrollis from down the street. Melanie practically
pulled her in by her lapels, then slammed and locked
the door behind her.

"What in the world...?" the little brunette exclaimed.

"I'm sorry." Melanie reached out to realign the
lapels of Joan's navy blazer. "I just didn't want...
Oh, never mind. Did I miss anything at the association meeting the other night?"

Joan and her husband Nick, both CPAs, had been
the co-treasurers of the Channing Square Residents
Association since its founding. Melanie liked the
forty-ish woman and appreciated her no-nonsense
style not to mention the precision with which she kept
the association's books.

"No," she said, "you didn't miss a thing, but if
you haven't been next door yet, you're missing the
boat. Have you seen your new neighbor?" Joan
sounded as breathless as a teenybopper.

"Briefly," Melanie said, wondering if that was actually drool beginning to form in a corner of the
woman's mouth. Good grief.

"Hubba, hubba." Joan rolled her eyes and poked
Melanie's arm with her elbow.

"Excuse me?"

"I said, hubba, hubba. You know, as in the man is
majorly attractive."

"Oh." He wasn't that major, Melanie thought sul-
lenly.

Joan gave a little sigh. "Well, I just wanted to give

you a heads-up before he's swamped by invitations from all the single women around here. And I wanted to thank you, too, you devious little bureaucrat.''

Melanie blinked. ''Thank me?''

''For seeing that the first Cop on the Block is ours, of course. Nice going, Melanie. You didn't waste any time. I can't tell you how much we all really appreciate it.''

''Oh. Well…''

Now, wishing it had occurred to her to do something devious, such as rushing through the paperwork for some nice, balding sergeant and his family of five, Melanie waved goodbye to Joan while she cast a furtive glance next door.

Then she stepped back inside and locked herself in. Permanently. She'd been looking forward to making pasta for the first dinner of her leave of absence and to enjoying what would be just about her last glass of wine for the next nine months. Now, with her perfect evening in a shambles, she ate a grudging bowl of cold cereal, then climbed into bed at eight, in the hope that she'd wake up in the morning to discover this was just a terrible dream.

Instead, she woke up shortly after midnight to the sounds of a party next door.

Sonny pulled an ice-cold beer from the cooler, snapped off the cap, and lifted the bottle in a toast.

''Hey, with warm friends and wet beer, who needs electricity or plumbing, right? Thanks, guys.''

When a dozen or so candlelit faces grinned back

at him, Sonny had to swallow a lump in his throat. For such a hardass, he was getting pretty soft and mushy these days, he thought as he sidled out of the front room and made his way toward the kitchen and a moment of solitude rather than blubbering in front of his colleagues.

He'd only told Kaczinski and one or two others about the house, but at least forty people had shown up over the past few hours for the surprise house-warming. It was heartwarming, too, because he'd been working alone and undercover so long he'd actually forgotten how many friends he had in the department after nearly thirteen years.

A few new neighbors had dropped in, too, but not the neighbor he loved. Mel had doused all her lights about eight o'clock. Then, around midnight when the volume of the party went up a couple notches, he noticed a bit of yellow light seeping through the shutters of one of the upstairs windows next door.

It wouldn't have surprised Sonny if she'd called the cops when things got a little noisy, but then on second thought she'd been peeking out the window enough to realize that most of the cops in the Third Precinct were already here.

Most importantly, he was here and alive after the incident last week that should have killed him. The DEA had asked for local backup on a raid on a meth lab in a desolate block on Sixteenth. Since Sonny was familiar with the area and the layouts of most of the abandoned buildings there, he was the first one through the door of the defunct auto dealership.

Normally, when he worked undercover, he didn't wear a vest. But that day somebody had tossed him one, saying, "This could get ugly." He'd shrugged into the heavy blue garment just before kicking in the front door and walking into the wrong end of a .44 Magnum and the path of a cop-killer bullet.

The damned thing had blown him backward through the dealership's dirty plate-glass window, practically out onto the street. He remembered lying there, in all that broken glass, looking up at a bright blue sky and thinking it was a shame that he was dead because all of a sudden he knew how badly he'd screwed up with Melanie and he realized just what he needed to do to fix things. If ever somebody had craved a do-over, it was Sonny just then.

As it turned out, when the bullets had stopped flying and the dust had settled, he hadn't been dead or even that badly injured. The impact of the bullet had cracked a rib and the subsequent collision with the pavement outside had given him a concussion. Maybe that was good. Maybe he'd needed a brutal jab to his heart and a thorough shaking of his head to see things straight. Now all he had to do was convince his ex-wife that he was no longer the selfish son of a bitch who had ruined their marriage.

"There you are." Mike Kaczinski came up beside him. He set the candle he was carrying down on the counter next to the sink. "You feeling okay, Son?"

"Oh, sure."

"How's the rib?"

"Fine." Sonny shrugged. "It only hurts when I breathe."

"And the head?"

"That's fine, too. It only hurts when I think."

Mike chuckled softly. "Well, that shouldn't be a problem, then."

The candle flame barely cut the darkness around the two friends as they stood there side by side. They'd met in grade school, gotten in all the obligatory trouble together in high school, shared a room at college, and then finally cheered each other through the police academy. Mike had been Sonny's best man, not just at his wedding, but in every sense of the word.

Like Sonny, he wore his dark brown hair on the long side, the better to blend in on the street. Unlike Sonny, he'd gone home every night to a solid, happy marriage for the past ten years.

Now the two of them stood shoulder to shoulder, looking out the window at the rectangle of yellow light on the second floor next door.

"She's planning to get pregnant next week from a freaking sperm bank." Sonny's voice barely rose above a rough whisper.

"Yeah. I heard."

"I'm not going to let that happen, Mikey."

"Yeah. I figured."

When the last reveler drove off into the wee small hours of the morning, Melanie slipped back into bed, beat her pillow to a pulp, and pulled the covers up over her head. Okay. So she wasn't going to wake up in the morning to find it was all a bad dream. It was a living nightmare, and she was going to have to deal with it one way or another.

She'd be damned if she'd stay barricaded behind locked doors. Sonny was just going to have to move. Seattle would be nice. Hong Kong would be even better. A bit closer, there was a house around the corner on Garland Boulevard that Dieter Weist and his partner had almost completed so Sonny wouldn't have to be bothered with all the drudgery that went along with rehabing. He didn't know the first thing about rehabing anyway. Good grief. When she'd lived with him in his loft, he hadn't even owned a screwdriver or a hammer to put a picture up on a wall, much less known how to use either one.

What was he planning to do? Live in that hovel next door while plaster rained down on his head and garbage squished under his feet?

He didn't even have electricity yet, for heaven's sake. No plumbing, either, judging from the Day-Glo-colored Porta Potty that she had spied tucked behind the dilapidated back porch.

Why was he doing this? She wanted to rip open the shutters and wrench up the window and scream, "It's over. It didn't work, Sonny. Just—for God's sake—let it go."

If she did that, though, he'd only yell back, "You love me, Mel. You know it."

Dammit. She punched the pillow again and dug herself deeper into the mattress. That was the problem. She did love him. She just couldn't live with him.

If only she'd known that when he'd handed her those two glasses of champagne and then shucked his disguise like some gorgeous butterfly emerging from a hairy cocoon. If only his voice with its too-much-whiskey and too-many-smokes timbre hadn't sent a cascade of tingles down her spine when he'd called her darlin' the first time, as in "Let's get out of here, darlin'."

Melanie was far too practical, way too levelheaded to be swept off her feet, so she'd finally come to the conclusion that Sonny must have drugged her those few weeks before they'd gotten married. That first night, after they'd left the awards ceremony and after he'd showered and changed at the precinct, they'd sat in the back booth of a little jazz club, the sparks between them nearly setting the place on fire.

No one had ever made her feel like the molten center of the universe before. No one had ever made her forget what time it was, what day it was, what century. No one had ever gotten her into bed on the very first date and then gotten her to stay there for an entire weekend.

He had to have drugged her.

It wasn't just the sex. During those early weeks Sonny had made her feel like a new person, somebody completely recreated. She'd never once made a list of any kind. She'd barely even opened her planner except to make certain there was no official function that would prevent her from being with her man.

Sonny had been with her constantly—24/7 as they said in the department—because, like now, he'd been on vacation following a shooting. He'd been sexy and funny and charming and attentive and sweet and…

…And in her drugged, delirious condition she'd married him one afternoon at city hall in Judge Beckmann's chambers with Sam Venneman as her maid of honor and Mike Kaczinski as his best man.

Then Sonny's time off work had ended and she'd hardly seen him anymore. It seemed her then-new husband's view of the ideal marriage was one where he worked long hours, sometimes two and three days at a time, undercover on the street, then came home expecting the honeymoon to continue under the covers with his irritated bride.

No sooner had she tidied up his messy loft than he stumbled in to fling newspapers everywhere, to put T-shirts in his sock drawer, to rip out the neatly tucked covers from the foot of the mattress to accommodate his long legs, to claim he couldn't make plans for the future because he didn't even know what he'd be doing next week.

She'd made lists and Sonny had made excuses.

After six months, during four of which she'd had a headache that felt like a cannonball inside her skull, Melanie had walked out and filed for divorce.

For his part, Sonny went through an approximation of the Five Stages of Grief. Denial: ''There's nothing wrong with our marriage, babe.'' Anger: ''What the hell do you think you're doing?'' Bargaining: ''I can change, Mel.'' Depression: ''Aw, hell, darlin'. Why don't you just stick a knife in my heart and get it over with?''

Finally, or so she'd thought when he'd stopped calling her constantly and dropping by city hall every other day, he'd reached the last stage. Acceptance.

Obviously she'd been wrong about that. Sonny hadn't changed a bit. He never would. He'd always be his spur-of-the-moment, let-the-devil-take-tomorrow, what-me-worry, haphazard self. And she'd always be the worrier, the list maker, the Queen of Post-It notes and the planner.

The twain would never meet.

And one of the twain, dammit, would have to go.

Melanie squeezed her eyes closed, determined to wrench at least a few hours sleep from the chaos that suddenly surrounded her.

Next door, at that precise moment, Sonny took a swig from his bottle of beer and a long drag on his cigarette, then leaned back his head and closed his eyes. He'd kept a couple candles burning to ward off any lowlife who might be looking for an unoccupied place to crash for the night. If that warning didn't prove successful, he was still wearing his shoulder holster with his service pistol snug under his arm.

He was almost hoping some coked-up derelict did stumble in, thus offering him a legitimate excuse to shove somebody up against a wall and work off some of the foul mood he was in.

Cop on the Block at your service, ma'am. What was that? You say you want a baby?

Every time he thought about what Melanie planned to do, his gut churned, tying itself into a thousand tight little knots, and his heart surged with a sort of primitive rage. It made him nuts to think of his wife getting pregnant by another man, artificially or otherwise. If otherwise, at least he'd have the pleasure of killing the guy. What could he do about the artificial deal—stomp a little vial and grind it into the floor?

He'd found out about her cockamamie plan last week, the same afternoon he'd gone through the plate-glass window. That revelation, coupled with the one he'd had from the .44 Magnum, had finally propelled him into action. Waiting for Mel to change her mind obviously wasn't working, and merely telling her that he'd changed wasn't good enough or fast enough in light of this baby deal.

The Cop on the Block notion had seemed inspired at the time. He filled out the paperwork, sat on his captain's desk until he signed it, then personally walked it through the approval process at the Third Street Bank. If the nerdy little vice president in charge of loans filed a complaint, Sonny was fully prepared to say that he'd simply drawn his gun to make certain the safety was on.

So far, so good. The house was his. He was sitting here, a mere twenty feet from Melanie's place. Of course, he was sitting in the dark and his toilet was outside and Mel was barricaded behind locked doors, but—by God—he was here. Now he just had to convince her that he was capable of change.

As for Mel, she didn't have to change even so much as a hair for him. He'd probably fallen for her the first time he'd seen her up on the stage at that awards ceremony exerting nearly superhuman effort to keep her knees together in that tiny little gray skirt while two hundred pairs of eyes were zeroing in on them and two hundred good but lecherous souls were silently pleading for just one little peek.

Okay. Maybe at first it was just the challenge of those lovely, super-glued knees. But after an hour of being with her that night, Sonny had quickly forgotten about the knees in order to focus on her quick, bright, and almost comically organized mind. And though he might have teased her about the lists and date books she produced from her handbag like a succession of clowns from a midget car, a part of him—an important, bone-deep part—truly envied the order and apparent certainty in her life.

Until Mel, the women he'd been with had lives as erratic as his own. Sheila, the flight attendant. Tammy, the traveling sales rep. Barb and Cathy and the other Cathy, all cops, all the time. Maybe the haphazard attitude was a habit with him, acquired from too many moves as a kid from one foster home to another. Maybe it was a defense. If he didn't make plans, they couldn't go wrong. Who knew?

But Sonny knew that from the minute he'd met Melanie Sears, he'd felt as if he'd found a permanent home. Then, because he continued to be an erratic, undependable, insensitive jerk, he'd promptly lost her.

He would've cut off his right arm for a second chance. Or quit smoking. *Really* quit this time. Whatever Mel wanted. Anything.

All she had to do was ask.

Assuming she ever spoke to him again.

In the meantime, he'd made his own list. After ''Get Melanie Back'' came ''Fix up this freaking dump.'' He drained the last of his beer, dropped his cigarette into the wet remnants in the bottle, then prayed he could slide into a few hours of dreamless sleep.

Chapter 3

There was no wake-up call in the world quite like the squeal of the hydraulic lift on a big flatbed as it prepared to slide a boxcar-size Dumpster onto a concrete pad.

Melanie groaned her way out of bed, snarled through her shower, and then got dressed and stomped downstairs to fix breakfast. She was starving after eating just a skimpy bowl of cereal the night before.

Sometime during the course of the night—sometime between the raucous hooting and door slamming of the party and the ground-shaking thud of the Dumpster bin shortly after dawn—she had decided to not let Sonny Randle ruin her life. Twice. If he couldn't accept the fact that their marriage was over, that was his problem. Not hers. If he wanted to waste his time trying to convince her otherwise, it wasn't going to work.

She had plans, and she was going to follow through with them no matter who moved in next door. Anyway, dammit, she was here first.

Muttering to herself, she pulled a box of eggs and a carton of orange juice from the refrigerator. She wasn't going to quit eating right just because Sonny was here. Of all the times in her life that good nutrition was important, it was now, prior to her pregnancy. She wasn't going to alter a lifetime's worth of good habits just because the King of Chaos had moved into the neighborhood.

As if to emphasize her steely resolve, she cracked an egg so hard against the edge of the bowl that it splattered across the shiny white tile counter and dribbled down the front of the oak cabinet. She didn't feel the least bit guilty blaming that on Sonny, too, as she grabbed a paper towel to clean it up. In fact, whatever went wrong from here on out would clearly be his fault if for no other reason than sheer proximity.

While she ate her scrambled egg with neat little bites of whole wheat toast, Melanie did what she did best. She made a list. Even if she decided to postpone Monday's appointment until next month, there were a million things that needed to be done. These weren't tasks she'd overlooked, but ones she'd saved for this special time. It was how she'd planned to spend her pregnancy, indulging herself in getting ready for the birth.

The nursery, on the second floor adjacent to her room, needed everything. She couldn't wait to shop for the crib and the dresser and the sweet little nightlight that would adorn it, but those would only come after she painted the walls the perfect shade of yellow that she had yet to find. Not daffodil. And it wasn't quite pale lemon sherbet, either. The best way she could describe the color in her head was baby-duck yellow. Melanie wrote that at the top of her list. Surely someone at the paint store would know exactly what she meant and be able to mix up a batch with ease.

She wrote down brushes, rollers, and paint tray, then decided that was probably enough for one day's To Do list. After all, she didn't want to finish everything in the first month and then have nothing to do for the next eight.

After she rinsed her breakfast dishes, she peeked out the window to see if the coast was clear enough to sneak out and get the morning paper. The big red sandstone house next door looked just as deserted as it ever had. The Cop on the Block, she supposed, was somewhere in the debris, sleeping off the effects of his orgy last night.

Melanie opened her front door and stood on her front steps a moment, stretching her arms toward the cloudless azure sky, then gazing at the pink-and-white blossoms of the dogwood trees in Channing Park. Next April on a lovely morning just like this one, she couldn't help but think, she'd be bundling the baby in a stroller and heading off for a lovely turn around the park. One more reason, she thought, to not cancel Monday's procedure.

There were always joggers and power walkers and just plain amblers moving at their individual paces around the park. Right now Melanie could see the Wrenn sisters coming down Kassing at a pretty good clip. She waved, hoping if they paused to chat, she didn't mix up their names the way she usually did. One was Susan and the other Sandy, but she was never quite sure which. There was only a year between them but they looked like identical twenty-something twins, both tall and terribly blond, and tended to dress that way, no doubt thoroughly enjoying the confusion they created. This morning they were wearing jiggly little T-shirts and a thin coating of hot-pink Spandex on their long legs.

She didn't have to worry about their names, though. As they passed on the sidewalk in front of her yard, both sisters waved and called in chirpy unison, "Hi, Melody," getting her name wrong as they always did. Then, without slowing, they continued on to 1224 where they quite suddenly put on the brakes.

"Hi, there," Susan or Sandy purred.

"Hi, there," Sandy or Susan echoed.

"Morning, ladies."

That voice! That sandpapery baritone with its top notes of booze and tobacco nearly brought Melanie to her knees. One quick glance revealed her ex-husband, a vision in a faded denim shirt and jeans, lolling on the little front porch next door as if he actually belonged there.

While he was chatting up the Wrenns, Melanie stalked down the walk for her paper. It wasn't on the walk, or under her little boxwood hedge, or anywhere to be seen. It was when she turned back toward her house and cast another furtive glance in Sonny's direction that she realized he was sitting there with the sports section draped over his knee. The son of a bitch stole her newspaper!

The minute Susan and Sandy cooed "Nice meeting you" and got under way again, Melanie yelled, "Is that my paper?"

"I borrowed it to look at the Classifieds," he called back.

She chewed on a few prime curses before she shouted, "Well, are you done?"

"Almost." He picked up the paper and disappeared behind it, apparently without the slightest intention of returning it to her in the near future.

God! Nobody on the planet could set her hair on fire the way Sonny did. She knew she should've shrugged with monumental indifference and sauntered back inside her house, but instead she clenched her fists and went charging across her yard toward his.

"Give me my damn paper," she shrieked as she pounded up the little flight of stairs to his porch. But just as she reached to grab it from his hands, Sonny stood and held the paper high over his head.

"Just a minute, Mel. I want to see if my ad is in here."

She glared at him. Not that she cared one bit or

was even mildly curious, but she still heard herself asking, "What ad?"

Sonny was looking up now, squinting in order to read the paper high over his head and well out of her reach. "This ad," he said. "Good. They got it in."

Melanie was gearing up for a leap worthy of a W.N.B.A. superstar when he suddenly snapped the paper closed and handed it to her. "What ad?" she asked again.

"I'm selling my car."

He lowered himself onto the thick sandstone blocks that formed the sidewall of the small porch while Melanie continued to stand. She wasn't at all sure that she'd heard him right. He'd had that gas-swilling, evil, black vehicle forever. It wasn't just transportation. It was his alter ego, as much a part of him as his sea-colored eyes and his devastating smile.

"You're selling the Corvette?"

"Yep." He leaned back against the house and slung a jean's-clad leg up onto the porch wall. "You were right. It's not a family car."

She blinked. "You don't *have* a family, Sonny."

"Not yet." He cocked his head, squinting against the morning sun at Melanie's back, but nevertheless pinning her with eyes that had turned a deep and warm Bahamian blue. "But I'm working on it."

"Well, I wish you'd work on it someplace else." She let go of an exasperated sigh as she plopped down on the top step. Her anger seemed to suddenly fizzle out, frustration taking its place. "This is crazy, Sonny. Buying this house. Pretending to be a docile

Cop on the Block when you're nothing of the sort, not to mention pretending to be Joe Homeowner.''

"I'm not pretending."

She rolled her eyes. "Oh, please."

"I've changed, Mel. Honest to God. Just give me a chance to—"

"Stop. I don't want to hear this." As she spoke, without even being aware of it, she was rolling the classified pages into a tight little log. When Sonny reached out for her hand, she batted his away with her newly discovered weapon. "Don't. Just don't."

He held up his hands in a gesture of surrender, then grinned. "You're going to have to iron that paper before you read it, Felix. I know how much you hate wrinkled news."

That did it. She was mad again, and only partly because he was right. She despised it when anybody read the paper before she did and got the pages all misaligned and unwieldy and…well…just messy.

"I'll just take my wrinkled news and go home," she said, snatching up the rest of the paper he'd littered all over the porch. "And since you're the Cop on the Block, I don't think I should have to remind you that it's illegal to take someone else's property, Lieutenant Randle."

"It won't happen again," he said solemnly despite the twinkle in his eyes. She was halfway across the driveway when he called, "Hey, Mel."

Now what? "What?" she snapped.

"Got any plans for this afternoon?"

Did she have any plans? That was a little like asking the state of Idaho if it had any potatoes, wasn't it? "Yes, I do. Why?"

"I need to drop the 'Vette off at Stover's Garage. There's a kid up there who's going to detail it for me before I sell it. I wondered if you could give me a ride back."

She sighed. "Okay. But the only reason I'm doing it is because I don't think you're capable of letting that car out of your sight for more than two seconds. I'll believe it when I see it." She looked at her watch. "I'll pick you up at Stover's at eleven, Sonny. That doesn't mean eleven-ten or eleven-fifteen."

"Mel, darlin', eleven to you means ten forty-five. I'll be there."

"I doubt it," she muttered under her breath.

At ten forty-five, true to his word, Sonny was out in front of Stover's Garage, watching the Saturday traffic on Grant Parkway for Melanie's little Miata. He chuckled to himself, thinking how he'd raised her hackles with the newspaper this morning. It hadn't been intentional. He'd planned to read the ads, then press every seam and fold before slipping the whole thing back into its plastic sleeve and tossing it onto her front walk.

Still, he had to admit he kind of enjoyed her snit. It had been a while since he'd seen one. Not that he found all of her quibbles and quirks endearing, particularly the virgin newspaper one, but they all stemmed from the part of her he loved and needed so desperately in his life. She was as beautiful and predictable as the sunrise, and he'd spent way too many years alone in the dark.

And as much as he needed her stability, she needed him to loosen her up, to raise those hackles of hers and ruffle her pretty feathers once in a while so they didn't harden in concrete. Damned if she'd acknowledge it, though.

He looked over his shoulder at his car—low slung, black as Darth Vader and twice as dangerous—parked on the garage's back lot between a wimpy turquoise Neon and a hulking Chevy Suburban. For a second he was tempted to snatch his key off the pegboard in the back room, start the throaty engine, and peel out onto the parkway after laying down ten feet of rubber in a desperate attempt to recapture his youth. But why he wanted to do that was a mystery. His youth had sucked. So had his entire life until Melanie had come into it.

He reached into his shirt pocket for a cigarette and was lighting it just as familiar voice nearby said, "Hey, Lieutenant, babe. Long time no see. What you up to these days?"

Sonny had a network of snitches all over the city that was the envy of every cop in every precinct. Hookers and pushers and thugs. Dime-bag men with dollar grudges. Disenchanted gang bangers. Snoopy grandmas who spent their days glued to their front windows. Some of them knew him as a vice cop. To others he was just a guy out hustling on the streets like everybody else.

Walking toward him now in a halter top and short

shorts and on high platform shoes was a young woman he knew only as Lovey. She wasn't much over twenty and had huge, sleepy amber eyes and skin the color of café au lait with enough needle tracks to make her a leading contender for Miss Pincushion. What a waste of a beautiful young woman.

"Hey, Lovey. How's it going?" He plucked another cigarette from his pocket, lit it, and handed it to her.

"Thanks, man." She reached out a long-nailed, slightly trembling hand for the proffered smoke, no doubt in need of a much more potent fix. "Hey. I heard you got shot."

"Nah. That was just a nasty rumor somebody started," Sonny said. "Or maybe wishful thinking."

"You got enemies, Lieutenant?"

"One or two," he said. "You know, that offer I made you a while back about the rehab program still stands. You interested?"

Lovey shrugged and inhaled so deeply there was hardly anything to exhale. "Maybe one of these days. You still in the market for information about Slink Kinnison?"

Was he! He'd been trying for more than five years to pin something that would stick to that scumbag and send him away so he couldn't get any more sixth and seventh graders hooked on his locally made and often lethal meth. Last week's raid hadn't put a dent in the guy's operation. If anything, it probably gratified him to have blown Sonny through a window.

Already reaching for his wallet and a couple of

twenties for Lovey's information, Sonny had to remind himself that he wasn't on the job right now,
which meant he wouldn't be reimbursed for the
money he laid out, no matter how important her information was.

A week ago he might have thought, What the hell,
it was only money, but now that he was a responsible
homeowner who needed every spare cent to rehabil-
itate his ancient dump, Sonny said, "I'm on vacation
for a couple weeks, but if you want to check with
Heilig or White down at the precinct, I'm sure they
can come up with a little something for you. You
know them, right? Heilig's the tall guy and White's
black. Here. I'll write down the precinct phone number for you and their extension.''

He patted his pockets to no avail. Where was a pen
when you needed one? "Do you have a pen and
something I can write on?'' he asked Lovey, who,
after a lengthy search, managed to produce a crumpled tissue and a stick of black eyeliner from her tiny
purse.

The tissue tore all to hell when he tried to scribble
the numbers and the thin black crayon broke. Just as
Sonny was swearing a blue streak, Melanie's little
yellow Miata pulled up at the curb. Out of habit, he
checked his watch and was shocked to see that it read
two minutes after eleven, which made her late for
maybe the second or third time in her entire thirty-
one years!

"Wait here," he told Lovey. "I know just where
I can get a pen and paper.''

He opened the passenger door, leaned inside, and couldn't restrain himself from saying, "You're late."

Melanie stabbed him to death with a look. "That's because I changed my mind about coming forty-eight times."

"I'm glad you came. Can I borrow a pen, Mel, and something to write on?"

It didn't surprise him to see her flip open the little center console and immediately produce a tiny spiral notebook with a tiny, color-coordinated pen clipped to its cover.

"Who's your friend?" she asked as she handed it to him.

"My snitch," he corrected. "I'll be right back."

While he wrote the phone numbers for Lovey, Sonny said, "After you talk to Heilig and White, you stay as far away from Slink Kinnison as you can, Lovey, okay? It probably wouldn't even hurt to leave town for a little while just to be on the safe side. Tell Heilig you need a little extra for bus fare. Is there any place you can go?"

The hooker shook her head. "Gotta stay close to my main man, Elijah. He takes care of me. He takes good care of all of his girls. You know?"

He knew only too well how her main man took care of her, by keeping her higher than a kite. Over the years Sonny had come to the bitter conclusion that the only thing wrong with prostitution was the pimps. Lovey's was Elijah Biggs, who weighed four hundred pounds when he wasn't wearing fifty pounds of gold jewelry and whose license plate proclaimed Bigg

Man. One of these days Sonny was going to see that
the big man got a one-way ticket to the state peniten-
tiary instead of always using the revolving door of
the city jail.

"Here." He flipped to a clean page in the little
notebook. "Here's my cell phone number and my
new address, just in case." He tore off both pages
and gave them to her.

Lovey studied the numbers a moment. "You move
into one of those big old ugly places on Channing
Square? What'd you want to do that for?"

"I don't know. I must be crazy."

She angled her head toward Melanie's car at the
curb. "That's your lady?"

"Yep."

"She live in Channing Square, too?"

"Yep. Next door."

"Next door!" Lovey laughed. "Well, that explains
why you're crazy, then. I'll see you around, Lieutenant."

"You be careful, Lovey."

"All the time, honey. All the time."

By the time Sonny slung his long legs into her little
car, Melanie was wishing she'd changed her mind
forty-nine times instead of forty-eight. That way she
would've stood him up instead of having to sit and
watch him do the job he did so damn well.

He wasn't one of those cops who got off on being
the long, hard arm of the law, who wore a badge and
a constant smirk, and felt entitled to push people

around if they dared get in his way. Sonny honestly believed he was making the city a better and safer place, day by day, person by person. She could tell from the expression on his snitch's face that the woman not only felt safe with him, but adored him, as well.

And if she knew her ex-husband at all, she knew he had probably just given the woman his phone number and told her to call him anytime, day or night.

"I thought you were on vacation," Melanie said as she angled her car back into the flow of traffic.

"I am."

"So, what's with the snitch?"

"Nothing," he said. "She just needed a little advice."

"I guess you're aware that the city's not responsible or in any way liable for actions or expenses of officers when they're on leave." She knew her words had come out in an annoying, almost schoolmarmish tone, but she couldn't help it.

Sonny just laughed. "I'll bet you've got a copy of the city code in your handbag."

"I do not."

"In the glove compartment, then."

Still laughing, he reached forward to open it, and Melanie swatted at his hand.

He turned to face her as much as his seat belt and the confines of the car would allow. "I guess you're aware that I've been on the job for over thirteen years now, and despite my charming and lackadaisical air, I do have some idea what the hell I'm doing."

"I know, but… Oh, damn." She slapped the palm of her hand against the steering wheel.

"What?"

"I just missed the turn onto Channing. Now I'll have to circle around and that'll make me late. Dammit, Sonny. It's all your fault."

"Late for what?"

"The hardware store."

"You have an appointment at the hardware store?"

She took her eyes off the road long enough to pitch him her most irritated look. "No, I don't have an *appointment*. I just wanted to be there by eleven-fifteen."

He looked at his watch and said, "Well, I'll tell you what. It's eleven-oh-eight right now. If we forget about dropping me off at the house and just head straight to the hardware store, we can be there by quarter after."

Braking for a red light, Melanie turned her head to her right. Sonny was sitting there, his knees up against the dashboard and the world's most innocent expression on his face. "'We'?" she asked.

"Yeah. I needed to go to the hardware store anyway. This'll save me a trip later. Then I can take you out to lunch when we're finished. Maybe to Dominic's or that new place down on Jefferson. What do you say, Mel?"

What did she say? To herself Melanie said she should have seen this coming. Give Sonny an inch and he immediately wanted a mile. How could she have been such a jerk? Knowing him as well as she did, how could she have allowed him to blindside her like this? Why was she letting him rattle her so?

"No problem," she said, trying to sound as if she meant it, as if his mere presence didn't faze her in the least. "I'll take you to the hardware store. But I'll pass on the lunch. Thanks, anyway."

Sonny had forgotten that shopping with Melanie was the equivalent of attending a nitpicker's convention. Even before they got in the store, she had to wait for just the right spot to open up in Dandy Andy's parking lot.

"Pull in over there," he'd said, pointing out an open space up ahead of them.

"Too narrow."

"How 'bout over there? There's plenty of room."

"Are you kidding me? Next to a twenty-year-old beater with dents in its door?"

Well, hell. It didn't make any difference to him where she parked or how long it took her to do it. He was just happy to be this close.

Once inside the store, Melanie whipped a list out of her purse and studied it gravely for a moment before she said, "This ought to take me about twenty minutes. Half an hour at the most. Shall I meet you up here in front or out by the car?"

"Whatever." He said it on purpose just to watch her eyes kind of pinwheel and her tongue hit the back of her teeth with an irritated little cluck. "Up here is fine."

"Do you have a lot to get?" she asked as she pulled a shopping cart from its nest.

"Well. Yeah. Everything." He nearly laughed watching her try to keep the top of her head on and the steam from pouring out of her dainty nose and delicate ears. "How 'bout if I just tag along behind you and pick up stuff as I go?"

"Suit yourself." She snapped her list taut and took off with a little snort.

Still trying to not laugh, Sonny wrenched his own cart from the row and followed in her wake. There was nothing quite like Mel's fine, firm, denim-cheeked wake. Ah, damn. How he wanted to reach out for a perfect handful of her.

The momentary attack of lust made him think about the imminent baby business, and his stomach knotted up again. Since this was Saturday, that didn't leave much time till Monday and the damned artificial deal. If he couldn't get her to even go to lunch with him, how the hell was he going to convince her to let him impregnate her?

Because he would. Sonny knew that as well as he knew his own name. Mel would've been pregnant the very first time they'd made love two years ago if they hadn't used precautions. Two bodies didn't come to-gether the way theirs did and not set life in motion. Two people didn't send sparks off the way they did and not start a fire someplace. If he was certain of anything, it was that.

He caught up with Melanie in the paint aisle. "What're you planning to paint?" he asked.

· "The nursery," she answered chirpily, sending his stomach into acid overdrive. He felt like throwing up, so he leaned his forearms on his cart and bent his head while Melanie accosted the paint guy with one of her typical opening remarks guaranteed to send a poor, overworked and underpaid salesclerk's eyes pinwheeling.

"I've got a very specific shade of yellow in my head," she said.

"In your head," the guy replied with a smirk in his voice.

Sonny didn't even want to see the one on his face because then he'd have to do something about it.

Oblivious to the kid's rudeness, Melanie pressed on. "I didn't see the exact shade on any of those little swatches. Maybe I could try to describe it for you."

"Ho-kay," the kid said somewhere between a yawn and a groan.

"It's not as bright as a jonquil," Melanie said. "And not as soft as lemon sherbet. I guess maybe there's a bit more gold in it than green. What I'm imagining is a baby-duck yellow."

The kid could barely restrain a guffaw. "Baby-duck yellow."

"Well, yes. That's how I imagine it."

While she went on at excruciating length, Sonny contemplated a few of the color swatches in the display case on his left. Who knew there were so many shades of white? Arctic white. Swiss white. Rice. Ice. Mel wasn't so far off the mark with her ditzy name, he decided.

"You sure you don't want a baby-chick yellow, lady?"

"No." She was adamant but sincere, as only Melanie could be. God bless her. "That's too yellow. Way too soft. Baby duck is exactly the shade."

"What about baby canary?"

The clerk's sarcasm sailed right over her pretty, precise head. "No. That's too soft, too."

"Ho-kay. How about baby-piss yellow? Or maybe…"

That did it, dammit. Sonny had the kid's narrow shoulders pinned up against the paint machine in two seconds flat. "Are you deaf, pal? The lady said baby-duck yellow."

"Y-yessir." His face had gone a perfect shade of Arctic white.

"You think you can mix her up some of that?"

"Y-yessir."

"All right, then." Sonny loosened his grip on the lapels of the helpful orange jacket. "How much do you need, Mel? A quart? A gallon?" he asked over his shoulder.

There was no answer.

"Mel?"

When Sonny turned to look, Melanie was gone.

If she'd had any spine at all, Melanie thought, she'd jump in her car and leave Sonny in the dust the same way she'd left him in the paint aisle. She looked over her shoulder in time to see him come out of the hardware store, pause just long enough to light a cig-arette, and then continue toward her.

Melanie picked up her pace, but even so Sonny reached the Miata before she did.

"What the hell did you think you were doing in there?" she yelled at him.

"What do you mean, what was I doing?" he yelled back. "Nobody talks to my wife that way."

She wanted to rip her hair out in frustration. "I'm not your *wife.*"

"Well, you should be, goddammit."

"Sonny, you…" Melanie closed her mouth. Not only were they being gawked at by passersby, but they'd had this argument before at least a thousand times. What was it Sonny didn't understand about the word divorce?

"Just get in the car," she told him. "I'm taking you home and then I hope I never see you again. Never ever ever."

She slid behind the wheel and jabbed her key in the ignition while she waited for him to get in.

"Mel, I—"

"Don't say it. I don't want to hear it. It was a simple trip to the hardware store to get paint and you had to turn it into World War III."

"I lost my temper," he said almost sheepishly.

But there was nothing remotely sheepish in her voice when she replied, "That's too bad, Sonny, be-cause you know what? You'll probably never find it again, either, in that chaos you call your life."

She jammed the car in gear, then turned up the radio so she couldn't hear him anymore.

Chapter 4

Melanie wasn't even sure how long she'd been sitting in the nursery, rocking in the maple rocker, staring at the unpainted drywall. Daylight had disappeared, and the little room was lit only by some stray light from the hall.

Her stomach growled angrily to remind her that she hadn't eaten either lunch or dinner. She might never eat again.

What a mess. What a horrible, freaking mess. There was no way she could deliberately or in all good conscience begin a pregnancy under so much stress. So, once again, she decided to cancel Monday.

She had to. It was one thing to say she intended to ignore the menace next door, but to actually do so was proving impossible. Sonny had spent the day hauling one load of trash after another out of the house and pitching it into the huge garbage bin in his driveway. Every time Melanie peeked out the window she cursed herself and promised she wouldn't do it again, but twenty minutes later—when she heard a crash or a thump outside—she'd find herself at a window, peeking out.

For a guy who claimed to be so distraught and distressed about the breakup of his marriage, he struck her as pretty cheerful. She heard him whistling half the time he was hauling trash. He paused to pat stray dogs and to chat with neighbors who bore house-warming gifts and, more often than not, while he chatted, he'd gesture toward her house. Melanie would have to jump back from the window so nobody saw her.

When Mike Kaczinski had stopped by with Connie and the kids, Melanie had hardly been able to tear herself away from the window. Oh, God. Little Michael had grown a foot and the baby, Jacob, was walking! It was all she could do to not run over there and grab up that little bundle of baby fat and giggles. Instead, she stood there like a spy and watched Sonny do it.

Damn him. He'd never paid all that much attention to the Kaczinski kids before so she suspected he was merely putting on a show for her, playing Daddy the same way he was playing Herbert Housekeeper and Cop on the Block. He was pretending to toss baby Jacob into the trash bin, and every time he swung him toward it, the little guy would squeal with glee. Each time Sonny stopped, Jacob would beg for more.

"More, Unca Summy. More."

Melanie finally had to turn away, not because she was afraid to be seen, but because it was breaking her heart and making her have second thoughts about canceling her appointment. She wanted her baby in nine months. Not ten.

She'd waited too long already. At thirty-one she was just barely under the wire for planning two pregnancies without things being dicey because of her age.

Aside from his chaotic lifestyle, that was probably the real reason she'd walked out on Sonny. "Let's wait a couple years, Mel," he'd say whenever she broached the subject of having a child. Or he'd brush her off with, "As soon as I stop working on the street, okay?" Or, "There's time, babe. We've got all the time in the world."

Her stomach complained again, and this time Melanie decided she'd best give it a little food before it shriveled up like a pitiful raisin. She gave a last, forlorn look at the bare, baby-duckless walls and then started down the stairs just as the doorbell rang.

With her jaw clenched like a vise, she almost couldn't ask, "Yes? Who is it?"

Through the door she heard, "It's Dieter, *liebchen.* So sorry I'm so late."

Dieter? Late? And then she remembered! Oh, Lord. Dieter Weist was to come at seven for a glass of wine and a consult on some architectural changes she was contemplating up in the playroom. She didn't want to insult the prize-winning designer by telling him she'd completely forgotten, so she slapped a bright smile on her face, opened the door, and welcomed him in.

Sonny glared at the silver Porsche parked in front of Melanie's house when he could no longer glare at the tall Nordic type who'd parked it there a while ago before sauntering up the walk and ringing the doorbell. If this was a date, they were taking their sweet, damned time getting it under way. He checked his watch. Sven or Hans or whoever he was had been in there an awfully long time. Close to half an hour.

In the months since their divorce had been final, Melanie hadn't had all that many dates, and those that she'd had, she hadn't enjoyed one bit. At least not the ones when Sonny had tailed her.

There was the dinner at Reggio's and the James Bond movie afterward with that vanilla-ice-cream news anchor from Channel Twelve when Mel could barely stifle her yawns. Sonny could hardly bear watching her that night because she'd been wearing the same gray suit, the one with the little scrap of skirt that she'd worn when he'd fallen for her. The news anchor appeared to appreciate it, too, and seemed sincerely wounded when Mel hadn't invited him in for a nightcap.

Then there was the concert at Emlin Hall with some lawyer old enough to be her father where she'd actually nodded off for a good five or six minutes. She hadn't invited that old codger in for a nightcap, either.

The one and only nightcap occurred when she'd

gone out with Bryan Bast, the real estate wonder boy, who'd somehow enticed her back to his downtown penthouse after an evening on the town. She'd stayed for half an hour and looked as if she'd been nursing a headache when she'd left.

She'd had a couple dinners with Sam Venneman, but Sonny hadn't even bothered to surveil those. Oversexed Sam needed Melanie's talents and organizational skills far more in city hall than he needed them in bed, so His Honor wouldn't have dared to put any moves on her outside of work.

But this Sven guy was a new player, a complete unknown. Not for long, though. Sonny called the precinct and asked Cathie Powers to run a quick make on the Porsche's plates. After she called him back, he stood staring out the kitchen window, nursing a headache of his own.

Who the hell was Dieter Weist and why was he still inside Melanie's house after all this time? Just when exactly was the big blond bozo planning to leave?

"You're walking a pretty fine line between surveillance and stalking, don't you think, Son?" Mike had said to him as they'd stood right here the night before.

But just as quickly as Sonny recalled those words, he pushed them out of his consciousness. He wasn't stalking her, for crissake. She was his wife.

"I see they've sold the house next door," Dieter said as he leaned forward to drag a broccoli floret through the dip that Melanie had thrown together. "Have you met the owners yet?"

"It's our new Cop on the Block," she answered without going into the grisly details.

Although she'd spent an incredible amount of time with this man when he was supervising the work on her house, she didn't really consider him a friend. Dieter was sweet with his graying blond hair tied back in a ponytail and his blue eyes framed by wire-rimmed glasses, but he wasn't someone to whom she could pour out her troubles. Anyway, the architect probably had enough troubles of his own, she guessed, since rumor had it that his longtime house-mate, Kevin, had just moved elsewhere.

"Really!" he exclaimed. "Good for you, *liebchen*. How did you manage to get us at the top of the list?"

"I didn't, actually. It was simple good luck." Melanie took another sip of her wine to wash down the lie.

"Well, that should make you even more comfortable with your decision about having the little one." Dieter licked a dab of mayo from his finger. "With a policeman next door, you won't even need an alarm system. All you have to do is open a window and yoo-hoo."

She managed a tight smile while he contemplated the vegetables again, this time choosing a carrot.

"So, Monday's the big day?" he asked, immersing the carrot stick in the pale green dip.

Melanie nodded. For the moment, at least, her on-again, off-again pregnancy was on. "I've still got so much to do to get ready. The nursery isn't even painted yet. Dieter, let me ask you something.''

''Anything.''

''Can you imagine a shade called baby-duck yellow?''

He didn't even snicker. The man regarded her with his frank blue eyes and said, ''Of course. I see it as a pale, pale gold. Is that the color you chose for the nursery?''

''Yes. Yes, it is.'' Melanie popped a crisp, plump bud of cauliflower in her mouth and chewed it almost smugly.

''Excellent choice, *liebchen,* especially since you don't know whether it will be a boy or a girl.''

''Thank you. Well, I don't want to take up too much of your time. I've made a list of some of the things I'd like to do with the playroom. Let me go and get it.''

''Good. Good. This is excellent dip, by the way. Scallions? Or did you use chives?''

''Scallions,'' she said over her shoulder on her way into the kitchen, thinking how she almost cut off her finger earlier while chopping the garlic and green onions for the dip because she was looking out the window more than at the cutting board. She looked out again now as she pulled her playroom list from a drawer.

It was hard to believe that Sonny hadn't lobbed a hand grenade at Dieter's car or done something else equally insane. The fact that his place was dark, without even candlelight shimmering through a dirty windowpane, didn't mean he wasn't there lurking. She was fairly certain that he'd followed her on a couple of dates in the past few months, but she couldn't prove it. No judge worth his robe would issue an order of restraint based on her flimsy, "Well, I just felt his eyes on me."

Dieter was waiting for her at the bottom of the staircase. "Any time you want to get rid of the Tabriz," he said, gesturing toward the deep blue and crimson Persian rug that ran up the stairs, "just let me know. It's quite nice. Didn't you tell me your parents bought it on their honeymoon?"

"My grandparents, actually. It is nice, isn't it?"

"You'll take it up, of course, until the little one isn't tempted to spill glue and grape juice on it."

"Why no!" She blinked. That had never occurred to her. In fact, she'd been intending just the opposite by leaving all of her expensive Persian carpets just where they were to cushion all of the baby's trips and stumbles just as they had cushioned hers when she was small. "I thought I'd leave them down."

He gave a tiny grimace. "That doesn't sound like you, Melanie. You're usually so careful and precise."

As she followed him up the stairs, she couldn't help but think that the man was right. It didn't sound like her at all, leaving a small fortune in textiles to the mercy of a little person guaranteed to throw up and have all sorts of wet accidents. It sounded more like something Sonny would do, and she wondered if his bad habits were crossing the driveway, marching like little black ants, to invade her house.

Ah, well. Maybe she would take the carpets up then. She'd put that on her To Do list.

By the time they climbed the narrow stairs to the third floor, Dieter was breathing a bit heavily.

"Well, let's take a look at what you want in here," he said, rubbing his hands together while he gazed around the huge empty space. "Let's see your list."

Melanie stretched out her hand automatically, but the list wasn't in it. Dammit. "Sorry. I must've left it downstairs," she said. "I'll be right back."

"Fine. No problem. I'll just wander around and see if I see anything." He clasped his hands behind his back and started pacing toward the tall dormers at the front of the house. "Sometimes ideas jump out from odd places."

Melanie trotted down two flights of stairs, found her list on the little Queen Anne table in the front hall, and hoped Dieter wasn't going to think she was crazy to want him to design and build a small stage with a proscenium arch on the north side of the playroom. She wanted one just like the one in the house where she'd grown up, where she'd spent so many magical hours at play.

But then again, maybe he wouldn't think it was crazy. Maybe he'd think it was sweet and charming. After all, the man hadn't laughed at her vision of baby-duck yellow. Unlike some others, he knew precisely what she meant.

She was on her way back upstairs when she heard Dieter bellow, *"Nein. Nein. Was is los?"*

Good Lord, what was wrong? Had he been attacked

by bats or spiders or something? Had he "seen" something horrible? Was there a ghost on the third floor? She quickened her step, but the big Bavarian nearly trampled her in his rush down.

"Dieter, what's wrong?"

"This is terrible," he said, barreling past her. "Fools! Idiots! Gestapo!"

It wasn't until she followed him out the front door that she realized why he was so upset. A police department tow truck, its lights flashing almost viciously, was backing up to his Porsche, preparing to tow it away.

"Nein. Nein. Halt. Was is los?"

Someone stepped from behind the truck to ask in a deep, familiar voice. "Are you the owner of this vehicle, sir?"

Sonny! My God, she should have known. Poor Dieter had been in the United States for more than thirty years and Lieutenant Sonny Randle, King of Chaos and Emperor of Aggravation, had just reduced the poor man to babbling in his native tongue. Lieutenant Randle was still wearing his denim shirt and jeans, but his badge was prominently displayed on his shirt pocket, not to mention the tough cop look so prominently displayed on his face.

"Ja, ja. It's my car."

"Well, I'm afraid it's parked too close to the fire hydrant, sir. We're going to have to tow it."

"Nein. Nein. It's my *car!"* Dieter wailed.

Melanie looked at the fire hydrant and mentally measured the distance to the Porsche's front bumper, concluding there was at least a foot to spare. "Sonny, you can't do this," she howled.

"Oh, no? Stand back and watch, babe," he said out of the corner of his mouth. "Hook 'er up, fellas," he called to the towing guys.

"*Nein!*"

Dieter practically threw himself across the hood of the little car. "Please don't take it, Officer. Let me move it. Please. *Bitte schoen*. I beg you."

"Well…" Sonny drawled.

"I have the keys right here." He dug in his trouser pocket and produced a jingling ring of keys. "See! I will move it away from the hydrant. *Ja?*"

Melanie stepped forward. "Dieter, you don't have to…"

"Shush," he told her brusquely. "I will handle this, Melanie. Please."

"Fine. Okay." Dismissed by the German, she threw an evil, it's-all-your-fault look at Sonny who seemed to be enjoying himself no end.

"Well, I guess I could let you off the hook just this once," he said, rubbing his jaw as if he were actually contemplating something. "But you can't just move it a foot or two. You're going to have to get that vehicle completely out of my sight."

"I can do that, Officer." The architect hurried around to the driver's door to unlock it. "It isn't a problem. I was just leaving anyway."

"Dieter!" Melanie protested. "What about…?"

"I'll call you," he said. "Next week. Thank you, Officer."

The Porsche's engine came to life, its headlights rose from their wells, and Dieter sped away while Sonny and his two tow truck cronies exchanged high fives and slapped one another on the back.

"You need us for anything else, Lieutenant?" one of them asked.

"That'll do it, guys. Thanks."

That did it, all right. Melanie was so furious she thought the top of her skull might actually blow off. "I could just kill you, Sonny," she shrieked.

"Careful, Mel. That could be considered threatening an officer of the law, you know." He grinned, a gorgeous white slash of a grin between the deep crevices beside his mouth. "I'm just doing my job, ma'am, keeping the community safe and the hydrants accessible in case of fire." He snapped a salute. "The Cop on the Block, at your service."

The fact that he looked so damned sexy just made her angrier. "You're ruining my life, Sonny Randle. In fact, ever since you moved in, I haven't *had* a life. I've hardly even eaten and my head hurts like hell."

Melanie spun on her heel and nearly ran back toward her front door, but she should have known that Sonny would get there first and block her entrance. Hot, furious tears burned her eyes.

"Get out of my way."

"Let me fix you dinner, babe." As he spoke he held up his hands to deflect her swats and slaps.

"No."

"Come on."

"No!"

He caught her hands in his and pulled her toward him, then lowered his voice close to a whisper. She could feel his warm breath at her temple when he said, "I screwed up, baby. Big time. I know that. But now I know how to do this right. How to do *us* right. Let me come in, Mel. Just to talk. Just for a little while." When he stopped speaking, his lips pressed against her hair in silent supplication.

"Oh, Sonny." Melanie leaned her forehead against his chest. "There's nothing to talk about. Can't you see that? Don't you understand? There is no *us* anymore."

"Okay. No us. Let's talk about you, then. Let's talk about you and this baby business of yours."

Her chin snapped up. She had no idea he knew. "You know about that?"

He sighed roughly. "Honey, everybody in city government knows about it. Hell, everybody in town! If I hear one more joke about sperm banks, I'm going to have to start breaking heads."

"I, uh, I didn't realize you knew."

"Can we talk about it?" he asked softly.

She studied his face a moment, trying to get a fix on his attitude, not knowing exactly how to deal with this quieter, less aggressive side of him. There was something in his eyes—a sadness or a sorrow, perhaps even a pain—that she'd never seen before. Good Lord. He actually looked vulnerable.

"I'll talk about it," she said, "but I won't argue about it. My mind's made up."

"Just talk to me."

"All right."

She thought perhaps she owed him that, considering their marriage, no matter how brief, but the instant Melanie opened the door to let Sonny in, she was certain she'd regret it.

While Melanie disappeared into the kitchen or someplace at the back of the house, Sonny lowered himself onto the couch in the living room and glared at the platter of raw vegetables and the two half-empty glasses of wine.

Anger burned through him again and he had to swallow hard and clench his fists to keep from picking up all the remnants of his ex-wife's date and throwing them across the room.

Don't screw this up, he told himself again. *Don't lose your temper. Don't blow up.*

Easier said than done. If that big German had given him any lip, he would have had him spread-eagled and in cuffs before the guy could say Wiener schnitzel. Okay. So the Porsche was legally parked. So it was an abuse of his authority. So what? What was a lucky few inches from a fire hydrant compared to the next forty or fifty miserable years of Sonny's life?

Out of habit, he lit a cigarette, then—after a single puff—rather than rile Melanie any more than he already had, stabbed it out in the dirt of a potted plant and covered the butt with fallen leaves. Leaning back, he dragged in a long, calming breath. *Don't screw this up.* To further cool himself off, he gazed around the room, pausing on the familiar objects that had briefly decorated his loft and his life.

Her dad's stained-glass lamp cast a jeweled light around the room, and his watercolors and oils ranged across the walls like old friends Sonny hadn't seen in a while. There was her collection of blue-and-white porcelain strategically placed on bookshelves where—God bless her!—all the volumes sat in alphabetical order.

That never made sense to him. Books ought to be grouped according to subject matter or by author, maybe even according to size. Melanie'd just looked at him as if he were crazy when he'd suggested that. She'd laughed and said, "When was the last time you looked at your bookcase, Sonny?"

He wasn't an organized person. Hell, compared to Mel, who was? As a kid, it was hard to be organized when he didn't know what foster family he'd be living with from one week to the next. As a cop, there was no such thing as regular hours or a typical day.

But there *was* a certain order to his life even if it wasn't visible to the naked eye. He didn't need to alphabetize everything to know how to find it. He didn't have to color coordinate his closet to know what to wear, and he didn't have to constantly make lists to know what he had to do.

He checked his watch. Right now, in the next thirty-six hours, he had to convince Melanie that there was most definitely still an *us,* and that one of the us was about to make a huge, irrevocable mistake.

* * *

In the little powder room off the kitchen, Melanie splashed cold water on her face and then dragged a brush through her hair in preparation for the inevitable battle with the man who couldn't take no for an answer.

She was annoyed with herself for telling anybody at city hall about her baby plans. City government was like a small town unto itself where news, both good and bad, spread like wildfire and where people were often burned by rumors that proved untrue. In light of that, Melanie had been candid about her pregnancy rather than have tongues start wagging about possible fathers of her child. Sonny, naturally, would have been right at the top of that list.

Right now, however, he was on her shit list. Glaring in the mirror, she decided her hair looked a little too good for the upcoming confrontation, so she frizzled it a bit with the brush before heading back to the living room, where her ex was looking just a tad too comfortable on the couch.

The light from the stained-glass lamp was turning his eyes a jewel green, casting shadows on his cheeks from his luxurious eyelashes. He seemed sleepy and sexy and far too content.

Melanie picked up the wineglasses on the coffee table, considered refilling hers, but decided against it because then she'd feel compelled to offer some to Sonny. He was hard enough to deal with when he was cold sober.

"Help yourself to veggies and dip," she said. "I'll take these out to the kitchen and be right back."

"Take your time," he said with an accompanying sigh. "This is nice, Mel. Really comfortable."

"Thanks." *But don't get too comfortable,* she thought. *And whatever you do, don't start remembering all the times we made love on that couch in that lovely stained-glass glow.*

Naturally, then, while she rinsed the glasses, those incredible moments on the couch were all she could think about. Of all the things that had deteriorated during their marriage, sex wasn't one of them. Sonny was an inspired lover. The unpredictability that drove Melanie so crazy out of bed was a distinct pleasure *in* bed. Or on the couch. On or under the dining room table. In the shower.

She felt her temperature rise a few distinct degrees, and blamed it on the warm rinse water coursing over her hands. What was it Peg had said to her? It was a shame to be having artificial insemination when Sonny was the genuine article. Well, if that meant a rock-hard body and the constitution of an ox, maybe so, but there was always that moment when the genuine article muttered a gruff little curse and put everything on hold while he reached for genuine protection.

There was no denying she missed sleeping with him. In the year since their divorce not one man had managed to elevate her temperature much less turn her on. That was okay. If it happened one day, that would be fine. In the meantime, the artificial article more than served her purpose.

Still postponing her return to the living room, she

dried the wineglasses and put them back in their proper place on the top shelf of the cabinet. She was still on tiptoe when she felt a pair of warm hands at her waist.

"God, I've missed you, Mel."

Sonny's voice was huskier than usual. Its deep tones sent a shiver down Melanie's spine even as the touch of his hands sent a shock wave through every bone and artery and nerve in her body. He stood so close behind her that she could feel his heart beating insistently against her back and the heat of his belt buckle and, below that, the strength of his arousal.

Don't. The admonishment echoed inside her head but wouldn't leave her lips.

Oh, don't. His palms slid up over her ribs while his lips tantalized her neck with whispered words of love. As much as Melanie wanted to scream for him to stop touching her, to stop kissing her, to stop professing his need, a part of her desperately longed for more.

Her stomach clenched and every drop of blood in her body seemed to thicken. Time seemed to halt completely. She couldn't help herself. She started to turn toward him just as a cell phone gave out a shrill beep.

Chapter 5

Sonny's cell phone beeped insistently.

"You need to answer that," Melanie said.

His lips tightened, but he didn't move his hands.

"Sonny! You need to answer that."

He swore viciously, and then nearly snapped his phone in two when he finally took the call.

"What?" he growled in place of hello.

Melanie edged away from him, almost deliriously grateful for the interruption. Otherwise...

She didn't even want to think about "otherwise."

While Sonny paced around the kitchen and talked with whoever was on the other end of the line, she returned to a neutral corner of the couch in the living room to sit with her arms clasped tightly across her chest while she berated herself for her astonishing, almost monumental lack of willpower. If the phone hadn't interrupted them… If it hadn't zapped her back to reality…

It was only now that Melanie realized just how vulnerable she was to her physical attraction for her ex. Out of sight, out of mind had worked reasonably well this past year, and the times when he was in her sight had been in public places with no possibility of intimate contact. She had even begun to believe that she was relatively immune to him, that her body was in total agreement with her practical head.

Now, sitting on the couch with every nerve end in her body sizzling and every synapse firing wildly, she realized just how wrong she'd been. The only reason she hadn't made love to Sonny this past year was that she hadn't had the opportunity.

It was fairly obvious now, given her nearly bestial attraction to the man and her appalling lack of control, that she couldn't allow herself to be alone with him in the future. Ever. She was going to kick him out of her house the second he got off the phone, and then she'd never let him cross the threshold again.

Just as she came to that conclusion, Sonny walked into the living room.

"You have to leave," she said, rising to confront him while infusing her voice with every milligram of iron in her body.

"I know, babe. Dammit. I'm sorry. One of my snitches is in trouble."

Four hours later Sonny checked his watch for the thousandth time. It was after midnight and the light, cold rain that had begun an hour ago was turning into a hell of a downpour. Lovey was nowhere around.

There had been stark fear in her voice when she'd called him to say that one of Slink Kinnison's pals had been going into the precinct tonight just as she was coming out after spilling her guts to Heilig and White for a paltry fifty bucks.

Hysterical, she had called Heilig from a phone around the corner, begging him to come get her and walk her into the building, past Slink's pal, in cuffs so it would look like she was there, again, under duress. But Heilig, who was about to go off duty, had basically told her to go play with herself. She'd called Sonny next, and he'd promised to meet her at the pool hall on Garrison, only the hooker hadn't shown up.

He'd looked for her everywhere, cruising the ten-square-block area that made up her usual stomping ground, even cruising past his own house a couple of times in case she was there. Melanie's lights had been on when he'd passed the first time, but her place was dark on his second and third passes, which was good, because if she waited up for him to return, she'd be in a blue-ribbon snit when he finally got there.

Who could blame her? He'd promised her that he'd changed, and then proved that he hadn't by leaving her in the lurch once again when the job beckoned. Way to go, Son.

The only good news was that she still wanted him. He'd had his doubts about that, and he'd halfway believed her when she'd told him he had no more effect on her physically than some stranger on the street.

But that wasn't true. He'd felt the way her body heated up beneath his hands. He'd heard the barely suppressed moan in her throat when he was about to kiss her.

Damn Lovey anyway for getting into a world of trouble at just the wrong moment, for calling him and then for not showing up. He wasn't going to one more sleazy dive or one more scuzzy shooting gallery in search of her. He'd cruise another fifteen minutes, that was all, and then he'd check out the bus station on the slim chance that she'd used her fifty bucks for a ticket. Then he was going home to try to figure out how to begin with Mel just where he'd left off earlier tonight.

At the bus station, the graveyard-shift employees were about as helpful as they usually were, which meant they hadn't seen anything or heard anything. The last bus had pulled out at twelve-fifteen and the next one wasn't scheduled until eight in the morning, so if Lovey wasn't already gone she wouldn't be going for another seven hours.

When he went back outside, there was a rain-slickered patrolman standing next to the Corvette.

"I figured this was yours, Lieutenant," the young cop said, rain pouring off the brim of his cap. "Just thought I'd keep an eye on your hubcaps while you were inside."

Sonny was so wet already he didn't even hurry to get in the car. "Thanks. I appreciate it. Have you been on this beat all evening, Patrolman...uh?" The kid's ID wasn't visible through his plastic rain gear.

"Moore, sir. Tim Moore. I've been patrolling between here and the stadium for the past four hours. It's been pretty quiet with the rain and all."

"I don't suppose you've seen one of Elijah Biggs's hookers around here. Tall, pretty girl with light skin and short reddish hair."

"You mean Lovey?"

"Yeah." Sonny's hopes rekindled. "Have you seen her?"

The cop nodded. "When I came on duty. She was at the precinct talking to Detective Heilig. I left before she did."

"Okay. Thanks, anyway. If you do happen to see her, tell her to get in touch with me, will you?"

"Sure thing."

"Great. Well, I guess I'll call it a night." Sonny walked around to the driver's side of his car and opened the door.

"Nice car, Lieutenant."

"Yeah, it is. It's for sale, Moore. You interested?"

"Oh, man. I'd take it off your hands in a hot minute if my wife would let me."

Sonny laughed. "I know what you mean, kid. See you around."

He drove back to Channing Square, hoping he'd find Lovey curled up like a lost, wet cat on his doorstep. When that turned out to not be the case, he decided she'd probably used her fifty bucks in snitch money to score some smack and had been blissed out somewhere the whole time he'd been looking for her.

The lights were still out at Melanie's, which was

probably a good thing considering how beat he was. He was almost too tired to take off his wet clothes, but he did, and then slung himself out on his mattress only to discover that the damned thing was soaked from a leak in the ceiling. He flipped it over to the dry side and dropped it a few feet away.

The odors of mildew and garbage settled over him in the darkness. His chest hurt where last week's bullet—the one with his name penciled on it—had ripped into the Kevlar vest. But despite his discomfort and exhaustion, sleep wouldn't come and his brain wouldn't quit nagging him.

That was an asinine thing to do, leaving Mel the way he had tonight just when he'd finally gotten close to her. Once again, he let the job take precedence over his personal life. Why did he keep doing that? Hell, when Lovey called Heilig at the precinct, he'd simply told her he was going off duty. Period. *Adiós. Vaya con Dios.* Good luck and God speed.

Sonny wasn't even sure he knew the meaning of "off duty." The job seemed to have permeated his bones, taken over his life completely. At least that was one of Mel's complaints during her abbreviated stint as Mrs. Sonny Randle.

He let go of a rough sigh, prompting his rib to complain, as well. What if he really hadn't changed? he wondered. What if the chunk of change he'd put down on this house, the mortgage, the ad in the paper for the Corvette were all just blowing smoke? What if it was all superficial, and underneath he hadn't changed one bit?

Time would tell, but he didn't have time. It was Sunday already, and Monday was coming at him like a runaway freight train on a downhill grade.

Monday his wife was going to conceive the off-spring of some wino who probably survived by sell-ing his blood every other week and his semen as often as possible. The idea of some stranger's child growing inside Melanie drove him nuts, but it was more than just that. It was far more than that. What if she and her baby shut him out of their lives? He couldn't even bear to think about that.

Okay. Relax, he told himself. *You blew it tonight, but there's still tomorrow.*

After that, there's the rest of your life.

The warm sunlight washed over her face when Melanie stepped outside early Sunday morning. Last night's rain had turned the park a vivid, gorgeous green. Even the street looked scrubbed and clean. Her paper was on the walk, right where it was supposed to be, and a furtive glance next door revealed only a vacant front porch.

So far, so good, she thought, heading down the sidewalk at a brisk pace. No sense tempting fate.

"Hi, Melody."

"Hi, Melody."

The Wrenn sisters emerged from behind a parked car. Their running garb was yellow today. Not exactly baby-duck, but closer to the shade used on warning signs for hazardous waste. It almost hurt her eyes to look at them.

"Hi, Susan. Hi, Sandy." Still uncertain which was which, she aimed the greeting right between them.

"Are you coming to the party tonight?" one of them asked while both of them jogged in place.

"Party?"

"The birthday bash," the other one said. "It's tonight."

Omigod. How could she have forgotten the annual Franklin Fayette Channing Birthday Blast, held each year to commemorate the man who'd originally deeded the park acreage to the city? This year she had even helped plan the party, which made forgetting it all the more disturbing.

"I'll be there," she said brightly, as if her mind hadn't slipped several crucial cogs.

"You don't happen to know if he'll be there, do you?" Susan asked.

"He who?"

They both looked toward the big red sandstone house and Sandy said, "Him. You know. The Cop on the Block."

"I haven't the slightest idea," Melanie answered.

The Wrenns turned toward each other. "Maybe nobody's invited him, Sandy."

"Maybe we should, Susan."

"Let's go," they echoed each other.

"Wait." Melanie held up a hand. "It's probably not a good idea to bother him this early. I heard his car pulling in really late last night."

Their perfectly made-up faces crumpled simultaneously. "Oh."

"I'm sure I'll see him later. I'll invite him then," she added, lying through her teeth, then cheerfully waving goodbye, tootle-oo, have a nice day as the beautiful, blond Wrenns jogged past Sonny's house without stopping.

Melanie snatched up the paper and went back inside where a fresh pot of coffee and a single, thawed wedge of iced pecan coffee cake awaited her. As always on Sunday morning, she extracted the editorial section from the paper to see what the critics had to say about city government this week. It wasn't easy reading, though, with one eye on the newsprint and one forever darting toward the window for a glimpse of the guy she'd almost gone to bed with last night.

She'd be lying if she denied it. If Sonny hadn't left of his own accord, if he'd argued and resumed touching her the way he had earlier, she'd have been a goner. Then she would have awakened hating herself this morning.

As it was, she wasn't all that wild about herself after *not* succumbing to his sexual charms. She felt on edge. Jittery. Tense. Oddly unfulfilled. Hell. She felt just plain horny.

She blamed her addled mental state on the hormones that Sonny had obviously stirred up. How could she have forgotten tonight's birthday bash when she had been the one to arrange the caterer and to address a hundred twenty-three invitations—in calligraphy, no less? She'd been looking forward to it for weeks, knowing it would be her last party before the pregnancy, kind of a swan song to her single lifestyle and a fanfare to imminent motherhood.

She even bought a new outfit specifically for to-night. A long, tiered denim skirt with the softest, most romantic white blouse. If she didn't wear them to-night, it would be a whole year before they'd fit again.

By God, she was going whether Sonny was there or not.

Still, it wouldn't hurt if she could head off anybody approaching his house who looked suspicious, as if they might be carrying a concealed invitation.

"Wait up, Mel. Where are you going?"

Damn. She thought she could sneak out to the car, start it, and back surreptitiously out of her driveway without being caught. No such luck.

"Out," she said, ignoring the black T-shirt molded to his chest and the faded jeans that adored—whoops, *adorned* his long legs. As he came closer, she also tried to ignore the worried creases around his eyes and the tautness around his mouth, always a sure sign of tension.

"Have you eaten breakfast yet?" he asked.

"Yep." She opened the door on the driver's side, but it closed when Sonny leaned a hip against it.

"I'm sorry about last night, babe." His voice rum-bled in its deeper registers.

"No big deal."

"One of my snitches was in trouble and I—"

"You really don't have to explain, Sonny." She

waved a hand, dismissing his apology, careful to not touch him for fear of catching fire again.

"I really have changed, Mel. Or at least I'm trying."

"Fine. Good for you. Congratulations. It just doesn't have anything to do with me, Sonny. How many times do I have to tell you?"

While he was ripping his fingers through his hair in frustration, Melanie spied one of the Wrenns out of the corner of her eye. God, those women were persistent!

"Get in the car," she told Sonny.

"What?"

"Get in the stupid car. I thought you wanted to take me to breakfast."

He practically vaulted over the Miata's hood and was in the passenger seat as quickly as Melanie could get behind the wheel. She started the engine, threw the stick in reverse, and watched Susan or Sandy leap out of her way as she backed out of the driveway.

It wasn't until she was making the turn onto Channing that it occurred to her that, to prevent Sonny from being at the party tonight, she'd just agreed to go out to breakfast with him.

"I'm glad you changed your mind, Mel." He sent one of his warmest, most dazzling smiles across to her side of the car.

Good God. Was it possible for hormones to actually eat away brain matter? she wondered. She felt as if she'd lost at least twenty or thirty IQ points in the past twenty-four hours.

* * *

Sonny wasn't exactly sure what Mel was up to, but as long as he was sitting next to her in a cozy booth at the Pancake Palace, he really didn't care. She looked almost as tired as he felt. Her blue eyes lacked their usual sparkle, and there were soft blue smudges beneath them that made him suspect she hadn't slept much last night. That made two of them.

"You've hardly touched your waffle," he said, pointing his fork at her plate. His own was nearly licked clean, he'd been so hungry.

"Here." She exchanged hers for his. "I don't know how you can consume so much food, Sonny, and not weigh five thousand pounds."

"I burn it off, I guess."

"I guess you do." A sudden smile appeared and her eyes sparked just a bit. "Do you remember when...? Oh, forget it. Never mind."

"What?"

"I was just thinking about the time we went to the reception for Governor Ziele and you ate an entire tray of rumaki."

"Those little bacon deals?" he asked between bites of waffle. "They were great. Do you remember—?"

"No."

"Wait a minute. You don't even know what I was going to say."

"It doesn't matter. I don't want to remember." She picked up the napkin from her lap and did a quick but precise pass over her no-longer-smiling lips, then folded it perfectly and tucked it under his empty plate. "Are you almost done? I really need to get going."

They reached for the check at the same instant. Sonny had to tamp down on his natural instinct to capture her hand in his, which slowed him down just enough to let Melanie grab the check. He finished the last of the waffle while she put on her invisible green eyeshade and recalculated the total.

Same old Mel. She hadn't changed a bit since she'd left him. Hell, maybe he hadn't, either. Not really. Not enough.

Out in the parking lot, he let her walk a few feet ahead of him so that he could enjoy the view of her shiny hair swinging just above her shoulders and the little twitch of her backside that always signaled she had places to go, people to see, things to do, all in a particular order. When she got to the car, she reached casually into her handbag, then swore as she began to rummage around inside it.

"Dammit." She started putting things on the Miata's yellow hood. Her wallet. A checkbook. A pink comb. A small leatherbound planner with a pen nestled in a leather loop.

"What are you doing, Mel?"

"I can't find my keys." She said it in the same tone that Chicken Little might have used to announce, "The sky is falling."

"You probably left them in the restaurant," Sonny suggested.

"I never do that."

As it turned out, that's exactly what she had done.

The cashier held up the key ring and jingled it the minute Sonny stepped back inside.

"I figured you'd be right back," the woman said. "This is the fourth set of keys this morning."

It was a first for Little Miss Perfect, though. It was almost a miracle. He whistled a happy little tune as he strolled back to the car where Melanie now had her head practically inside her purse.

"Keys," he said, dangling them above her.

"Oh. Thank God." She started tossing her belongings back into her bag in no particular order, then she held out her hand for the keys.

Sonny jingled them again. "Getting a little sloppy, aren't you, Mel?"

"It's your fault," she said. "You distracted me."

He lifted an eyebrow. "Oh, yeah? Was it my scintillating conversation or just my physical presence?"

"Neither." She snatched the key ring out of his hand. "It was the aura of chaos that always surrounds you. You make me crazy, Sonny."

"No," he drawled as he opened the door for her. "I make you human, Superwoman. You need me. You know you do."

Like a hole in the head, Melanie thought as she gunned the engine and turned out of the Pancake Palace's parking lot. A hole in her head through which everything—all her careful plans and best intentions—seemed to be leaking. Pretty soon her brain would simply dry up and blow away like so much gray dust. She'd just lost her keys. God only knew what would be next.

The worst part of it was that Sonny was right. She had a tendency to be a pill. Okay. A pain in the ass. Her own father had been the first to point that out when she was a mere eleven years old, or "eleven going on forty-two" as he'd put it.

"Relax, little girl," he used to say. "Life won't fall to pieces if you ease your grip on it a bit."

She knew that. At least she knew it in her head. Her heart was another matter. And she didn't need a shrink to tell her that her compulsive nature was likely the result of losing her mother at such a young age and being left in charge of her disorganized father.

And, dammit, every single person who considered her such a pill and a pain in the ass was always falling-down-kissing-her-feet grateful for her pillness when it rescued their sloppy, disorganized butts.

"How could I have left my keys?" she moaned as she gave the steering wheel a flat-handed slap.

"Better slow down a little here, Mel. The speed limit's thirty-five."

Her gaze dropped to the speedometer that was registering a healthy fifty-two. She eased off the accelerator at the same moment she realized she'd once again driven past Channing. Way past. They were already five blocks south.

She was tempted to blame her ex-husband again, but she knew it was her own fault for letting him in the car in the first place.

"I must be losing my marbles," she said, checking

the rearview mirror before flipping on the directional signal and pulling over to the curb. "You can get out here, Sonny. 'Bye. It's only a few blocks back to the square."

"Whoa. Wait a minute."

"Just get out, okay?"

He gave her one of his blue-eyed, Pound Puppy looks. "You're going to just kick me out of the car? Here?"

Melanie sighed. "Yes. Right here. If I take you all the way back, I'm going to be late."

"For what?" He chuckled. "More paint?"

"Yes, as a matter of fact." She didn't sound nearly as indignant as she felt. There was nothing wrong with knowing exactly what she wanted, then doing her very best to get it, for heaven's sake. "This paint is important to me."

"The baby-duck yellow."

"That's right," she snapped.

"Well, what if I told you I know a guy at a certain hardware store who claims to be the best paint mixer in town?"

"What guy?" she asked suspiciously. "What hardware store?"

He just smiled. Silently. All-knowingly. She really wanted to smack him.

"How do you know this guy?" she asked.

"He used to be one of my snitches. He was a house painter before he got busted for writing bad checks. Now he's on parole and works in a hardware store in the First Precinct."

"Okay. Okay. You win. You don't have to get out here. I'll drive you all the way back to the square. Where's this hardware store? How do I get there?"

Sonny shook his head at the same time he crossed his arms and kind of dug his shoulders into the seat-back. "I'm not sure I remember the exact address. It's really off the beaten path, Mel. I'll have to show you."

"You jerk."

"I'm just trying to help you, babe. This guy...I think his name is Jerry. Ol' Jer can whip you up a gallon of baby-duck yellow with both eyes closed and one hand tied behind his back. You'll see. Trust me."

"Take a left on Sutton, Mel." Sonny pointed up ahead in traffic. "Then it's about halfway down the block on the right."

At least he hoped so. It had been a couple of years since he'd had any dealings with Jerry What's-His-Name.

"This is a terrible neighborhood," Melanie said for the third time, each one increasingly nervous. She'd hit the switch to lock the Miata's doors half a mile back. "It's one of the ones on Sam's Blight Bill."

Sonny was thinking that he was going to be on *Mel's* Blight Bill if this didn't pan out. "There it is. You can park right in front, babe."

He unhooked his seat belt as soon as she killed the engine. "Wait here. I'll run in and see if Jerry's working today."

"But I..."

"Just wait, Mel. And lock the doors."

It was a terrible neighborhood. Sonny gave the entire block a quick once-over before entering the store. "Is Jerry around?" he asked the woman at the checkout counter. She rolled her eyes, pointed toward the back, and sighed, "What's he done now?"

He made his way down a crammed aisle, at the end of which stood an Elvis clone with a cigarette dangling from his snarling lips and enough grease on his hair to slide the *Titanic* out of dry dock. "Jerry?"

The guy blinked his hooded eyes. "Hey, Lieutenant."

"I need a favor," Sonny said, and after he'd explained about Melanie and the color in her head, he added, "There's a hundred in it for you if you can come up with the right color."

"Hey. No problem, man."

"It's perfect. I can't believe it. It's just the color I imagined."

All the way home, Melanie could hardly keep her eyes on the road. She kept glancing at the back seat where some of the paint—the perfect baby-duck yellow—had dripped down the side of the can. As much as it galled her to apologize to her ex-husband, she dredged one up.

"I'm sorry, Sonny. I honest to God thought you were just sending me on some wild-goose chase."

"A wild baby-duck chase, Mel." He gave her one of his best smiles. "I told you to trust me."

"Well, I guess I will. At least where paint is concerned." She turned into her driveway.

"What are you doing this afternoon?" he asked, in no apparent rush to get out of the car.

Melanie reached back for the gallon can. "I'm painting."

"Need some help?"

"No, thanks."

She got out of the car and started toward her back door. "Thanks again, Sonny."

"Sure. Glad to help. Guess I'll see you at the party tonight, huh?"

Melanie almost lost her grip on the can. She'd just spent half a day trying to keep him from being invited to the birthday bash, and he'd already been asked!

"These block parties are usually pretty dull affairs," she said, hoping to discourage him.

"Good," he said, cheerfully and horribly undeterred. "Fits right in with my new style."

Chapter 6

This was the fifteenth annual Franklin Fayette Channing Birthday Blast, and as always it was hosted by Jeffrey and Helene Savin, who were among the neighborhood's pioneer residents. Their Second Empire town house on Channing wasn't only huge and stately, it was the envy of anyone who had ever pulled up a floor or knocked down a wall or hauled tons of rubble from a dank hundred-twenty-year-old basement.

Helene Savin was one of the city's foremost interior decorators, and her home stood as the showcase of her talent and exquisite taste. It didn't hurt at all that Jeffrey had the money to indulge that fine taste. From the quarter rounds on the glossy parquet floors to the intricate moldings that hugged the twelve-foot ceilings, not a single detail had been overlooked.

Even the switchplates had been meticulously hand painted to match each room's décor. It was Melanie's kind of place.

She had planned to enjoy this party as a kind of send-off for her pregnancy. She had imagined herself savoring her final taste of wine while she discussed preschools and nannies and pediatricians with some of her female neighbors, women she didn't know all that well yet because her job at city hall left her with little free time and, up until now, she hadn't been interested in preschools and nannies and pediatricians. She had intended to change all that tonight.

But instead of the party being her salute to impending motherhood, it had turned out to be a celebration for the Cop on the Block.

"Good job, Melanie."

"We're just thrilled."

"We'll sleep better just knowing he's there."

"I'm looking forward to meeting him. Is he here yet?"

No, thank God.

After being congratulated by just about everyone in attendance, Melanie had finally positioned herself in a dim corner of the Savins' elegant music room from which she was able to train a wary eye on the foyer. If Sonny had already arrived, it hadn't been by the front door. She was certain of that.

"Helene outdid herself this year, don't you agree, *liebchen?*" Dieter attempted to juggle a wineglass and several canapés while he dragged a gilded folding chair close to Melanie's in the corner. "What are you doing back here in Siberia?"

"Hiding from my ex," she said. "You had the great misfortune of meeting him last night."

"*Ja,* I heard."

"I'm so sorry about what happened, Dieter."

He ate his last canapé and took a thoughtful sip of wine. "No need to apologize for him. No need at all. The man is obviously crazy for you."

"The man is obviously crazy period," she said, peering around the big Bavarian to check the foyer once more for new arrivals. "You haven't seen him this evening, have you?"

Dieter shook his head and glanced a bit nervously over his shoulder. "*Nein.* I saw him this afternoon at the Wrenns' house while I was out walking, but I immediately changed directions."

She tried to not look surprised, and hoped she was concealing her irritation when she asked, "What was he doing at the Wrenns'?"

"Well, to me it looked like he was checking windows. I thought that was one of the duties of the Cop on the Block. Checking homes to see if they are burglarproof or not."

It was. Melanie had written the guidelines herself, but she'd never in a million years imagined it would be Sonny checking out the Wrenns. Those two tootsies hadn't wasted any time taking advantage of his expertise. She wondered whether or not their windows and doors, along with their other parts, had passed muster.

"I think I'll wait a while before I request him to look at mine," the architect said. "I see you found the paint for the nursery."

"Excuse me?"

"The paint for the little one's room." He touched her hand. "You have yellow paint around your nails."

Melanie looked down. She hadn't even noticed it while she dressed for the party. Now, in addition to losing her mind, she was losing her eyesight.

Dieter finished the last of his wine in a single gulp. "I'm going back for some more of Helene's good Merlot. Can I bring you something, Melanie?"

"No, thanks."

After Dieter lumbered toward the bar that had been set up in the dining room, Melanie shrank back into her corner beside the perfectly groomed ficus in its big and expensive Chinese porcelain pot. She lifted her wineglass to her lips and then inspected the spot of yellow enamel decorating her right thumb. Sonny's paint maven, Jerry, claimed the only way he could come up with the perfect baby-duck yellow was with an oil-based paint rather than an easy latex, so Melanie had spent as much time cleaning up this afternoon as she'd spent painting one measly wall.

Wondering if wine would be as effective a paint remover as turpentine, she checked to see if anyone was looking and then dipped her finger in the glass and proceeded to rub her knuckle with a cocktail napkin. It was while she was doing this that she heard twin peals of laughter coming from the foyer.

There they were, Susan and Sandy Wrenn, in all their bottled-blond glory. They were dressed in skinny black leather pants, tiny white sweater sets, and chunky gold necklaces that advertised their prominent breasts—all four of them. They looked stunning, like twin statuettes, like gorgeous golden bookends. And Sonny was the book, the cheap, sleazy detective paperback, between them.

Melanie's heart performed a familiar little flutter, an ecstatic little flip, even as she edged her chair farther back behind the ficus. If she'd dreaded encountering Sonny earlier, she double dreaded it now when she was so…so… Well, she didn't know what she was, but a dozen emotions seemed to be churning inside her and some of them were undoubtedly playing across her face. The last thing in the world she wanted was for her ex to see how he unsettled her by his mere presence.

Knowing Sonny, he'd probably think she was jealous. That was probably why he'd made this late, great entrance with a Wrenn hanging on each arm. He'd done it on purpose, just to aggravate her, just to show her that even if she didn't want him, there were plenty of women who did. Or, if not on purpose, he'd accomplished it by the same haphazardry that ruled every other area of his life. But she wasn't jealous. Hardly.

Well, maybe a little. If she had to rank all the emotions she was feeling, she'd put jealousy fairly far down the list at number ten or eleven.

Melanie reached into her handbag for the little hand

mirror she always carried, hoping to reassure herself
that she didn't look like a recent escapee from an
asylum, but half expecting to see a face similar to one
of Picasso's portraits of women who were part serene
being and part crazed beast. The face that greeted her
in the mirror wasn't exactly serene, but it wasn't
Screaming Mimi, either.

"He is here, *liebchen*. Did you see?" Dieter had
to elbow a ficus branch out of his way before he could
sit beside her. "Here. You said you didn't want one,
but I thought maybe you could use a fresh Merlot."
He held out a full glass of wine.

"Thank you." Melanie polished off what was left
of hers, then traded her empty glass for the full one.
"Skoal," she said, clinking its rim against Dieter's
glass.

"Skoal," Dieter said.

From the other side of the ficus, a sandpapery baritone said, "Cheers. And Happy Birthday to Franklin
Fayette Channing."

Then two sopranos piped up.

"Hi, Melody."

"Hi, Melody."

When Herman the German made another trip to the
bar, the cheerleaders went with him—thank God!—
leaving Sonny alone with Mel for the first time that
evening. She looked so pretty in her long, soft skirt
and simple white blouse. Hell, she looked pretty in
anything. Or nothing.

"How'd the painting go?" he asked, flipping the

German's folding chair around and straddling it while he draped his forearms over its back.

"Fine," she said, conjuring up a tight smile and then taking another healthy gulp of red wine.

It was her second or third glass as far as Sonny could tell, and she was starting to show the effects. Melanie didn't get blitzed often. In fact, during the time he'd known her, it had only happened three or four times. But when she did, it was always the same. Instead of getting loose-limbed like the majority of drunks, Mel's posture stiffened until it was hard telling her from a bedpost. Instead of slurring her words, her speech became even more precise than usual. The dead giveaway, though, was when she started hand pressing her clothes while she was still wearing them.

"This is some house," Sonny said.

"Yes. It's lovely." The hand that wasn't gripping the wineglass smoothed her skirt across her leg, then moved to tend the sleeve of her white blouse.

"You missed a spot of paint on your finger, Mel."

"That's already been pointed out to me," she said. "Why don't you go circulate, Sonny? Everyone's dying to meet you."

"I'd rather stay here with you."

"Well, I'm leaving." She stood.

Sonny did, too. "I'll walk you home."

"No need."

She brushed past him and started to make her way toward the front door, weaving, wobbling every now and then, through groups of people who kept slowing her progress with their greetings and congratulations and requests to be introduced to the Cop on the Block. While Sonny followed a few steps behind her, she threw enough murderous looks over her shoulder to get herself arrested.

Their hostess was still at her post in the foyer. "You're not leaving, are you, Melanie?" the tall, gray-haired Helene Savin asked. "Sam was looking for you."

"Sam?" Melanie looked just a little confused rather than halfway in the bag.

"The mayor, darling," Helene said. "Wait here just a moment. I'll hunt him down."

She swept away in the direction of the bar, leaving Sonny and Melanie standing alone in the foyer.

"Sam's here," Melanie said, blinking as if a bright light were shining in her eyes. "I thought he wasn't coming. When I gave him the invitation, he said he had other plans for tonight. He did. I checked his calendar."

She was really talking to herself, but Sonny answered anyway. "Maybe he changed his mind. People do that, you know, Mel. Change their minds."

Since she didn't take offense, Sonny figured she probably hadn't even heard him, or that his remark had sailed right over her Merlot-soaked brain. She was still a bit wobbly, so he curved his arm lightly around her waist and planted his hip against hers to steady her just as Helene came back with Sam Venneman in tow.

"Here he is. I found him," she trilled.

The mayor looked as if he'd just come from a photo shoot for *GQ* in his beige raw-silk blazer, sharply creased slacks, and shiny tasseled shoes. He was perpetually tanned, but seemed even more so this evening. He stuck out a bronzed hand.

"Good to see you, Sonny."

Talking with a champion politician like Sam Venneman was always a weird experience for Sonny because, even though the man looked straight at him, Sam always seemed to have his antennae directed toward four or five other conversations taking place nearby.

"Good to see you, too, Sam," he said.

"They tell me you're our first Cop on the Block! How the hell did Melanie manage that?"

"She's pretty persuasive," Sonny said.

The mayor laughed. "Tell me about it. I don't know what I'm going to do without her for the next eighteen months." He turned to Melanie then. "Why didn't you tell me Sonny was up for the first mortgage loan in the program? I could have cut through some red tape for him."

She rolled her baby blues and muttered, "He seems to have cut through it pretty effectively all on his own."

"Good for you." Sam slapped Sonny on the back. "I didn't realize the two of you were back together."

A little gasp broke from Melanie's throat. "We're not," she said. But Sonny knew the politician hadn't heard her. Maybe his antenna was broken.

"So, Sonny, I guess you're looking forward to fatherhood?"

"Definitely." Sonny bit down on a grin. "I can't wait."

"Sam, you don't understand this at all," Melanie began very slowly and precisely. "We are not—"

She was interrupted by a blood-curdling scream.

"Can you see anything?" the mayor asked.

Melanie shook her head.

They were standing on the sidewalk in front of the Savins' house with a throng of partygoers, all of them straining to see across the street into the darkness of Channing Park. After a woman's scream had pierced the night, Sonny had gone flying outside and hadn't been seen since.

"It's been almost ten minutes now," Sam said, edging back his French cuff to consult his Rolex. "Are you certain someone put in a call to 9-1-1?"

"Helene did," Melanie said. "I think I hear sirens right now."

As worried as Sam appeared, Melanie was fairly sure it wasn't about Sonny or the poor victim in the park, whoever she was. The instant her scream was heard, His Honor had directed Melanie to find a phone—not to call 9-1-1, but rather to alert the mobile news crew at Channel Twelve. Their van with its satellite dish on top was just now coming down Channing. Sam strode out to the curb and waved. As Melanie well knew, her boss would do just about anything for film at eleven.

While the TV people were setting up, she wandered to the other side of the yard. The park was illuminated along its perimeter and around the bandstand, but the interior was mostly dark. Without a moon tonight, it was utterly black beyond the jogging and bike path.

"Sonny," she whispered, hardly aware that her lips had moved.

"This must be just awful for you, kiddo." Her neighbor, Joan Carrollis, slipped an arm around Melanie's shoulders and gave her a warm hug. "I wish you had told me Friday that our Cop on the Block was yours before I made that stupid *hubba, hubba* crack."

Melanie sighed. "It is awful. But he's not mine anymore. I just remembered this is one of the reasons I left him."

"Because of his job?"

She nodded. "Because when he left for work I never knew if he'd come home or not."

"I'm not sure I could cope with that, either," Joan said. "Kind of makes me glad I married a boring accountant."

Chewing on her lip, Melanie tried to see into the darkness across the street. Her mind felt foggy from the wine. Her head was beginning to ache. "I just wish I knew what was happening. I wish I could see something," she said. "Can you see anything, Joan?"

"Nothing."

Several squad cars had pulled up down the street. Their flashing lights felt like knives in Melanie's

head. She hadn't had a headache like this since her
divorce.

Then suddenly there was a shout—was it Sonny?—
and all of the various flashing lights, from the TV
crew and the patrolmen with flashlights and the high
beams on squad cars, seemed to converge on a little
group of dogwood trees across the way.

"Look!" Joan exclaimed. "There he is! He got
him!"

A man in jeans and a dark jacket was flattened
facedown on the petal-covered ground. Sonny knelt
above him with one knee planted in the guy's back
while he wrenched his arms back to cuff him.

"There's a woman by the bandstand," he shouted,
lifting a hand to shade his eyes from the glare of the
lights. "Get the EMTs in there right now."

Melanie felt her heart shift dramatically. She was
able to take in a deep breath now.

"Don't cry, sweetie," Joan said.

She didn't even realize she was.

There was nothing like a rape to put a damper on
a party. Most people didn't even go back in the
Savins' house, but drifted away from their yard once
the rapist was hustled away and the television lights
were turned off.

Melanie had found a quiet spot in which to hide in
the small formal garden at the side of the house. She
was angry at Sam Venneman for using another human
tragedy to further his career. She was angry at herself
for dissolving into useless tears. She was angry at

Sonny on general principle. If anybody spoke to her, she was sure she'd start screaming like a banshee.

"Ready to go, babe?" Sonny's open hand magically appeared in front of her. "I'll walk you home."

His knuckles were scraped. For some reason that made her feel like crying again. She couldn't even look at his face for fear of blubbering.

"You go ahead," she said.

"I'll wait," he said softly. "It's getting chilly." He shrugged out of his jacket, placed it around her shoulders, and then lowered himself onto the ground beside the wrought-iron bench where she sat.

Her body seemed to soak up the warmth remaining in his jacket. It smelled like him—male, athletic, just a touch of citrus from the aftershave he always wore. God, she used to breathe in huge lungfuls of him, just loving the way he smelled.

Melanie had forgotten how quiet Sonny could be when he sensed she didn't want to talk. Whatever other faults he had, he'd never invaded her private space. He may have teased her about her idiosyncrasies, but he'd never belittled her or tried to make her change. She couldn't quite say the same for herself, could she?

"I'm sorry, Sonny." Her voice sounded small and distant.

"For what, babe?"

"Oh, everything." She gripped the lapels of his jacket and pulled it closer around her, partly for its warmth, but mostly for its fragrance. "I'm sorry about us. It was my fault, too."

If she'd expected him to utter a little shout of victory or to offer her a smug "It's about time you admitted it," she was wrong. He hardly reacted at all.

"I thought that would please you," she said. "Hearing me admit it wasn't all your fault. You can gloat if you want."

"Maybe tomorrow."

There was something in his voice…

When she turned to look at him, she gasped. "Sonny, there's blood on your shirt. Oh, my God! On your pants, too."

"It's nothing," he said. "I just got nicked a couple times. The son of a bitch had a knife."

Melanie was up on her feet now. "You should have let the paramedics take a look at you. Why didn't you let them take care of you?"

"Well, first I had to get Sam and the idiots from Channel Twelve out of my face, and then I needed to find you to make sure you weren't going to walk home alone."

Earlier, during all the commotion that followed the arrest, she had watched Sam and the media people descend on Sonny like a plague of urban locusts. Idiots. Didn't they realize the stupidity, not to mention possible danger, of putting an undercover cop in the spotlight? Sam should have known better.

"Well, walk me home now," she said. "Come on. We'll get my car and go to the emergency room at Saint Michael's."

Sonny stood. "All I need is a Band-Aid, Mel."

"We'll see about that."

The park looked so pretty it was hard to believe something terrible had occurred there only an hour or so before. To Melanie's knowledge, there hadn't been a rape in the neighborhood in two or three years.

"I feel so sorry for that woman," she said. "Was she...?"

"He cut her pretty bad."

From his brusque tone, she could tell he didn't want to dwell on the subject. Lieutenant Sonny Randle never did bring work home. But then, he wasn't home all that much.

When they reached her front door, Melanie paused to shake her head just as she was about to insert her key in the lock. She almost laughed. "I can't believe I'm about to let you in here for the second time. Of my own free will!"

"Hey, if I had known getting stabbed would do the trick, I'd have put myself in the path of a crazed felon yesterday."

Once inside, Melanie turned on a few lights in addition to the ones she'd left burning during her absence. "Are you sure you don't need to go to the E.R.?"

"I'm sure," he said. "Really, Mel. It's just a few scratches."

"Okay. Well, then, I'm going to run upstairs to see what I've got in the medicine chest," she said, then only half in jest added, "Don't bleed all over my furniture."

"Aye, aye, Captain. Mind if I get something to drink from the kitchen?"

Already on her way up the stairs, she called back, "No. Go ahead. Help yourself."

This wouldn't be the first time she'd patched him up. Sonny might not have brought his problems home from work, but he'd brought home more than his share of cuts, scrapes, bruises, splinters and wrenched parts. Her first-aid skills, learned at a young age when she'd had to tend her klutzy, absentminded father, had improved dramatically during her brief marriage.

The contents of the medicine chest in the bathroom upstairs, unlike the contents of her bookcases and spice drawer and pantry, weren't alphabetized. The spacing of the glass shelves made it impossible to arrange the variously sized bottles and jars and tubes in anything resembling the proper order. To the average, non-compulsive human being, it might have looked quite orderly, but to Melanie the little cabinet was a mess. Every time she opened its mirrored door, she'd catch a fleeting glimpse of herself in full frown.

To compensate for the annoyance, she took what she needed in alphabetical order. Antibiotic cream. Band-Aids. Cotton balls. Gauze. Peroxide. In addition to those supplies, she grabbed a bath towel from the linen closet so the King of Chaos didn't get blood stains on her silk upholstery.

Instead of juggling her supplies, she wrapped them neatly in the towel and then trotted down the stairs. Halfway down, she called, "I hope you're not sitting on my silk sofa, Lieutenant."

When she turned the corner into the living room and saw her ex-husband standing there in nothing but his black silk briefs, the breath nearly chuffed out of her body. Dear God, she'd tried with all her might to forget those long, lovely muscles of his thighs, the corded calves, the impeccable pecs above the glorious abs. Her mouth went a little dry. She had to clear her throat before she spoke.

"Here. I brought you a towel so you don't get bloodstains on the sofa." She unpacked her first-aid supplies on the coffee table and handed him the towel, half hoping he'd wrap it around his waist, half hoping he wouldn't.

He hadn't worn sexy underwear when she'd met him. He'd worn wrinkled boxers with the plaids nearly laundered out of them. Then, for his birthday, almost as a joke, she gave him a pair of expensive black silk briefs. She thought they'd wind up wadded in the back of a dresser drawer, but not only had Sonny worn them, he'd promptly gone out and purchased several more pairs.

For a minute it seemed so warm Melanie thought she might have mistakenly turned the furnace on before she left for the party. She absolutely refused to believe that it was she who was turned on.

She grabbed up the bottle of peroxide and a fistful of cotton balls.

"Sit down, Sonny. Let's get this over with," she muttered.

Chapter 7

Sonny's breath hissed through his clenched teeth when Melanie dabbed the antiseptic on his leg.

"I swear to God, Mel, sometimes I think you use that prehistoric stuff specifically to torture me."

"Hush. It works, doesn't it? You're still alive."

"Barely," he mumbled.

He probably ought to be glad the son of a bitch in the park hadn't had a gun, Sonny thought. If he'd had his own, the guy would be in the emergency room now if not in the morgue. But he'd wanted to be truly off duty at tonight's party in hopes of convincing Mel that he wasn't a cop 24/7, that he could put the job aside and enjoy life's pleasures.

"This one isn't too deep," she said, tending the slash on his biceps now.

The stuff she used to clean it hurt worse than the

wound itself. Sonny leaned his head back and closed his eyes. This wasn't going the way he'd planned. Being in Melanie's house stripped to his skivvies was definitely on the evening's agenda, but not bleeding all over the place or feeling her light touch on his arm and his leg while knowing it was purely medicinal.

He heard himself swallow and realized he was still thirsty. He'd gone into the kitchen to get something to drink while Melanie was upstairs, but after he'd opened the refrigerator, looking for orange juice, he'd just stood there staring at the appliance's showroom-clean interior and its neatly arranged contents.

The ketchup bottle was wiped clean, without a trace of red residue around its cap. Same for the mustard. There was a bowl of glistening grapes. Nearby, the yogurts were lined up like little soldiers, and Sonny hadn't a doubt in the world that they were ranked by expiration date. All of the small plastic boxes on the top shelf were neatly aligned and labeled in Mel's tiny, tidy print.

Sometimes he missed her so much he couldn't even breathe.

"Do you think I'll live, doc?" he asked her as she pressed a bandage to his arm.

"This time," she said.

When she began gathering up the first aid stuff, Sonny stopped her with a hand on her back. "Sit here a minute. Talk to me."

She sighed. "What about? Because if..."

"Anything," he said. "The weather. Politics. Tell me what's going on at city hall."

She relaxed a little, leaning back, her arm just brushing his. "Just the same old Byzantine wheeling and dealing. The Board of Aldermen approved my program last week by a fairly stunning majority. But then you already know that."

His eyes were closed again. He was merely enjoying the sound of her voice. Deep for a woman. Sexy. Seriously sexy.

"It's a good program," he said. "You worked hard putting it together and getting everybody on board."

"I just hope it'll have some kind of effect on the crime rate. I don't know. Maybe I was overly optimistic when I projected that ten percent reduction. Maybe it's ludicrous to think that a few scattered off-duty cops can make such a difference."

"Well, it worked tonight. It didn't prevent the crime, but it sure as hell got one criminal off the streets."

She murmured in agreement, then they were both quiet for a minute. Sonny reached for her hand and was surprised she allowed him to clasp it in his. It surprised him, too, that that was all he wanted physically at the moment. Just to hold her hand. It was like coming in from the cold to sit in front of a warm fire.

After a moment she asked, "You're not really serious about this house business, are you?"

He turned his head toward her and opened his eyes. "You think I took out a thirty-year mortgage just for fun?"

"Well, no, but..."

"I'm serious, Mel. You just watch."

"You don't know the first thing about rehabing a house. It's a huge undertaking."

"I'll learn."

"It takes time, Sonny. Hundreds, even thousands of man hours. Your job barely even allows you to have a weekend off."

"I'm going to make some changes. Who knows? I might even put in for a desk job. There are a couple openings right now."

She rolled her eyes. "I'd like to have an oil portrait of you sitting at a desk for longer than six minutes."

"I might surprise you," he said.

"Well, go ahead. Do what you want. It really doesn't have anything to do with me anymore."

"It has everything to do with you." He brought her hand to his lips for a soft kiss. Sensing her resistance, he decided it was time to change the subject. Telling her he had changed really didn't count for squat. He was going to have to show her.

"How's your headache, babe?" he asked. "Want me to massage your neck?"

For just a second her gaze softened, then she shook her head. "No, thanks. I think I'll just go up to bed. I've got a big day tomorrow."

He tightened his grasp on her hand. "Mel…"

"It's late, Sonny." She pulled her hand away. "Please go."

One of the distinct disadvantages of being an organized person was that there was nothing to scrub or to wash or to rearrange in the wee small hours of the morning when, to keep from going totally nuts, a person really needed an all-consuming distraction. So, at two-thirty in the morning, Melanie was in the nursery and up to her elbows in baby-duck yellow.

Maybe if Sonny had put up more of a fight when she'd told him to go, she could have worked up some righteous indignation that would have made it easier for her to fall asleep. Maybe if he'd tried to kiss her while they'd been sitting on the sofa or when she'd walked him to the door, she could have slugged him and worked off some of her physical frustrations.

But she'd told him to go and he'd put on his clothes and gone home. Just like that.

God. Maybe he had changed. Maybe…

No.

Melanie slogged the roller through the tray again and swiped another wide swath of color on the drywall, trying to not remember that it was Sonny she had to thank for the perfect shade. She was also making a valiant effort to not remember the sight of his long, lean body clad in only a couple of Band-Aids and a few ounces of spun black silk.

It didn't strike her as very appropriate for a mother-to-be to be entertaining the lurid thoughts that kept popping up in her head. And it miffed her no end that while she'd sat there salivating tonight, Sonny hadn't reacted to her at all. For all the revealing silk revealed, she might as well have been his kindergarten teacher or just another needlepoint pillow on the sofa.

He'd certainly changed in that respect. During their

courtship and marriage, they'd never sat side-by-side on the sofa for any length of time without winding up horizontal someplace—either there on the sofa itself, or on the floor beside it. She wasn't at all sure what she would have done tonight if the opportunity, or Sonny, had arisen.

She stopped still with the roller halfway through its pass over the wall. Was he sick? Was there something physically wrong with him that he hadn't been able to tell her? Why else would he even contemplate taking a desk job unless he was no longer up to the rigors of being on the street?

He'd been hit by a bullet in that drug lab bust, but he'd been wearing a vest. From even the little she had read about the incident, he hadn't been seriously injured. And she'd seen enough of his bare skin tonight to know that, other than the new knife cuts, there were only the usual complement of scars.

Besides, if Sonny were seriously ill, she was sure he wouldn't hide it from her. What better ploy for getting her back than appealing to her conscience and her natural care-taking instincts?

She was the one who was going to be seriously ill if she didn't stop letting him upset her. She'd planned to get a good night's sleep before her appointment tomorrow, and here she was up painting at almost three o'clock.

My God. The appointment wasn't tomorrow anymore. Tomorrow was here already. It was today!

Sonny pitched another armload of trash into the Dumpster at the rear of his driveway. He'd been haul-

ing garbage and warped linoleum and broken glass
and God only knew what else for more than three
straight hours, and he'd barely made a dent in the
mess inside the big house. Whoever came up with the
term ''sweat equity'' was right on the mark. He was
soaked. Good thing they were turning on the water
today. At least he'd be able to wash up in his kitchen
sink.

Yesterday he'd driven to the precinct to take a
shower, but he couldn't do that today because, during
a break from hauling trash, he'd sold his car. As it
turned out, Patrolman Timothy Moore's wife had ca-
pitulated and given him permission to buy his dream
car. The kid hadn't even taken it on a test drive.

''If it's good enough for you, Lieutenant,'' he'd
said, ''I know it's good enough for me.''

''Well, if you have any problems, let me know,''
Sonny had told him, trying to sound macho and un-
sentimental. John Wayne saying so long to Ol' Paint.
Bogey dumping Bacall. ''Go on. Get going. Thanks
for the cash.''

It was just a car, for God's sake, he'd kept telling
himself when Moore drove away and that metallic
purr dwindled in the distance. What would he rather
have, Melanie or the 'Vette? Both, actually, but that
wasn't the right answer, dammit.

After the car was gone, he worked even harder.
Every time he walked outside with another load, he
looked for Mel, but there were still no signs of life at
1222. It wasn't like her to sleep late any day, but

especially not on one for which she had special plans. Of course, it wasn't like her to stay up until all hours the night before a special day, either. He'd watched the lights come on in the nursery last night and, when he'd finally dozed off around three, they were still blazing.

Her appointment was at eleven. It was written in big glossy red letters on her calendar in the kitchen. He saw it last night. Baby: 11:00.

Baby. The word broke from Sonny's lips like a curse.

He looked at his watch. It was ten-thirty now. Her gynecologist's office was all the way across town, which meant if she left right this minute, she'd have to race across the parking lot and take an express elevator to be in his waiting room at eleven, which meant that by Melanie's standards she was already fifteen minutes late.

Unless she'd changed her mind.

Unless she'd canceled the appointment.

He didn't realize he was holding his breath until he had to drag in a chestful of air. Just as he did, Mel came barreling out her back door.

"I am so late," she said to no one in particular as she sprinted for the Miata.

"Morning, Mel," he called, enjoying the way her black slacks molded to her legs as she moved, to say nothing of the white top that hugged her lovely, high-riding breasts. God, he loved looking at her.

"I'm late," she called back.

"Well, that's a first."

She had time enough to pitch him a murderous look before she slid behind the wheel and stabbed the key into the ignition. The switch ground but the engine didn't turn over. She turned the key again, this time making the ignition nearly scream. Still, the engine didn't respond. After her third try, Sonny sauntered over before she wreaked permanent damage to the vehicle.

He tapped on the driver's window. "Car won't start, huh?"

Even before the glass descended he could hear her blistering string of curses. Sad to say, she'd probably learned the worst of them during their time together.

"I can't believe this! Why won't it start?" She slapped her open palms on the steering wheel.

"Dunno. Pop the hood and I'll take a look."

She scanned the dashboard, then swore again. "I don't know where the... Oh, wait. Here."

The gas cap popped open. Sonny pressed it shut. "It's by your knee, Mel."

"Which knee? I have two."

"Your left."

She reached down. A second later the latch on the hood released with a little thunk.

"That's it," Sonny said. He checked the oil, mostly to look busy, then stood staring thoughtfully into the engine compartment when Melanie joined him.

"Can you tell what's wrong?" she asked.

He shook his head, then leaned forward to jiggle a wire. "Everything looks okay to me."

"Maybe it's the battery," she said as if she even knew where it was.

"Nope. I don't think so."

"Well, what is it?"

He shrugged. "Dunno."

She treated him to a whole new vocabulary of curses then, and kicked the front tire while she was at it. "I have an appointment at eleven o'clock," she wailed. "What am I going to do?"

Helpful neighbor that he was, he shrugged again.

"I know. I'll take the Corvette. Could I borrow it, Sonny? Just for an hour or two? I can have it back by one, I'm sure."

"Sorry, babe. It's gone."

"What do you mean, it's gone?"

"I sold it. The guy came by at eight this morning, took one look at it, and handed me a fistful of cash." He pulled the wad from his pocket as proof. "I was going to ask if I could borrow the Miata to take this to the bank."

"Oh, great." She threw up her hands. "This is just great."

"You could call Stover's Garage. Of course, they probably couldn't get anybody over here till this afternoon."

"Great," she snarled.

"Sorry."

"Well, okay. This isn't a disaster. It's not the end of the world," she said as if she were trying to convince herself of it. "I'll just have to shift my appoint-

ment. That's all. I'm going in right now and call.
Thanks for the help, Sonny."

"Sure. No problem."

"Would you like to reschedule for next week?"
the nasal voice on the phone asked.

"No, you don't understand," Melanie said. Good
Lord, how many times did she have to explain to this
woman. "This is for artificial insemination. It has to
be today or tomorrow. I can call a cab and be there
by eleven forty-five, I'm sure. Twelve at the latest."

"No," the woman said through her nose. It came
out sounding like *new*. "I'm afraid that's not possible.
Doctor is leaving on vacation at noon today. His last
appointment was at eleven."

"That's *my* appointment," Melanie shrieked.

"Would you like to reschedule for next week?
Doctor will be back in the office Thursday."

"Listen to me, you…" Melanie clenched her teeth.
"I'll have to call you back. I really can't even speak
right now." Other than to curse.

Melanie slammed the receiver back in its cradle.
During the conversation, she'd been pacing from one
end of the kitchen to the other, but now she pulled
out a chair and sat before she keeled over from blood
pressure that must have been over the moon. Okay.
It wasn't the end of the world. She'd be fertile in
another twenty-eight days. What was the worst that
could happen? She'd have an Aquarius instead of a
Capricorn. She'd adjust. Everything was the same—
just one month off.

It was tempting to blame this on Sonny, but it was her own fault for staying up so late painting and then forgetting to set her alarm. Of course, even if she hadn't been running late, the car still wouldn't have started and there wouldn't have been time enough for a cab.

Maybe she just wasn't meant to get pregnant today. She didn't really put much faith in astrology or other woo-woo things, but maybe in this case fate simply had other plans. Maybe it was for the best. Worst case she was going to have an extra month to get the nursery and the playroom ready. How bad was that?

Having talked herself out of a thoroughly rotten mood and lowered her blood pressure in the process, she went to the sink to get a glass of water and was just in time to see Sonny hoist another box of trash into the Dumpster. His denim shirt was dark with perspiration and his hair was falling over his forehead until he reached up to rake it back with his fingers.

He sold his car! She'd been so upset about her own car earlier that she hadn't even reacted to his astonishing news. Sonny sold the sleek, black, bad-ass, love-of-his-life Corvette. Good God. She didn't believe he'd actually do it.

She leaned closer to the window to peer down the driveway just in case he was lying and the Corvette was actually parked back there, hidden under a tarp or something. She looked back at Sonny, who was now standing with his arms crossed, gazing at the back of his house like a proud homeowner.

The world as she knew it seemed to have strayed drastically off course. Melanie went back to bed.

Sonny took a break at one o'clock. Lunch was a warm beer and a couple of granola bars. Sitting on his front porch, he gazed idly at the park across the street where several women were laughing and chatting as they pushed strollers along the perimeter path. They looked so happy, as if there were no better place in the world to be than Channing Park, and nothing better to be doing than pushing a kid ahead of them into a bright spring day.

He ticked off nine months on his fingertips. Mel planned her baby for January. He couldn't even begin to fathom all the reasons for that, but he knew she had them. She'd missed today's appointment, but she could still make her baby deadline. He'd be only too happy to oblige.

Before he approached her with a proposition, however, he was going to have to sneak the spark plug back under the hood of the Miata. If she caught him, and assuming she didn't kill him, she'd probably have him arrested for malicious mischief. That was okay. He was ready to go as far as kidnapping.

While he was watching the young mothers turn east on the path, an unmarked department car pulled up at the curb. Mike Kaczinski got out and ambled up the broken concrete of the sidewalk.

"Lunch?" he asked, eyeing the beer can and the granola bar wrappers.

Sonny aimed a thumb in the direction of the front door. "The beer's in the kitchen. Help yourself."

"I'll take a rain check. Thanks."

Mike was in street clothes, but it was obvious he was on duty. For a minute, Sonny felt like an unemployed bum trying to corrupt an officer of the law.

"How are things going down at the shop?" he asked. "Anybody miss me?"

Shaking his head, Mike edged a hip onto the porch wall. "Nah. We're all enjoying the quiet. The captain can't find anybody to yell at."

Sonny laughed.

"How's it going?" Mike's gaze slid toward the house next door.

"She missed her appointment this morning. Damned car wouldn't start."

"Shame," Mike murmured.

"Yeah." Sonny took a swig of beer. "Damned shame."

"Just don't step over the line, Son. You know what I mean?"

"I know what I'm doing, Mikey. Don't worry about it."

They'd been friends long enough to know that this particular discussion was temporarily closed.

"I heard you sold you car," Mike said, changing the subject to one almost as unpleasant. "What are you going to get to replace it?"

"I'm looking at a minivan."

His partner's eyes widened. "Jeez, Sonny. You really *are* serious about this."

"Nothing wrong with a minivan, pal."

"I didn't say that. Hey, I've got one myself." Mike snickered. "They build character."

Sonny took another sip of beer, wondering if it was too late to return Patrolman Moore's money. Probably.

"Nice going on that rape last night," Mike said. "Turned out the guy had a couple dozen priors. He's going away for a long time."

"That's good. This Cop on the Block deal might not be such a bad idea after all." As Sonny well knew, the thinking was otherwise in the department. The low-cost loans were great, but nobody thought it was going to make a damn bit of difference in the crime rate. Not that he was going to express that opinion to Mel, though.

"Hey, I ran into an old pal of yours yesterday. Elijah Biggs. He said to tell you to keep your nose out of his business. Well, he said it a little more colorfully than that, actually."

"I can imagine. He didn't happen to mention Lovey, did he? I was supposed to hook up with her a couple nights ago and she never showed up."

Mike shook his head. Just then the radio in his car gave out a garbled squawk. He sighed and stood. "No rest for the wicked, I guess. When's your vacation up, anyway? I don't like seeing my partner having so much damn fun on a Monday afternoon."

"Another week."

"Good. Oh, and I'm supposed to tell you to bring

Melanie for dinner just as soon as you get a rope around her.''

"Will do.''

Sonny sat watching Mike respond to his radio call, trying to not feel envious, pretending his own adrenaline wasn't kicking in when Mike slapped his red light on the hood and peeled away from the curb.

He finished his beer and the last granola bar, then went back to work, hauling the trash that seemed to be breeding faster than he could carry it out.

A little before six o'clock, after her long and wonderfully dreamless nap and before she called the garage to send a mechanic over first thing in the morning, Melanie tried to start her car again.

"I'll be damned,'' she muttered when she turned the key and the engine promptly caught and then idled without so much as a glitch. She sat there a moment, blinking, thinking that if this had happened seven and a half hours ago, if the car had started, she'd be pregnant right now. Her baby would be born in January and all her plans would fall into place like perfectly spaced dominoes.

But who knew? Maybe if her car had started, she might have been in a terrible accident on her way to the doctor's office—or worse, on her way home.

Not that she felt like belting out a chorus of "Que Sera, Sera,'' but Melanie was willing the accept the verdict of fate. There was something to be said, she supposed, for a February baby. Little Alex or Alexis would be ten months old at Christmas, perhaps even starting to walk. That would be nice.

"Hey! How'd you get the car started?"

Sonny was walking toward her, looking sexy as hell in jeans, a black T-shirt and a black wool blazer worn to conceal his shoulder holster. She didn't even want to imagine the scrap of black silk underneath. The total effect was I'm-not-a-drug-dealer-but-I-can-put-you-in-touch-with-one. She had always suspected that he was a frustrated actor since he played his undercover parts so well.

"I have no idea," she said. "All I did was turn the key and it started right up."

He leaned down, bracing his forearms on the window well. "You missed your appointment this morning, huh?"

"Yes." That was pretty much all she intended to say on the subject, so she hoped he wouldn't pursue it toward the inevitable argument.

He didn't, thank heavens. His response was to cock his head and offer her one of those deeply bracketed smiles that were always guaranteed to scare up a flock of butterflies in her stomach. His eyes turned that warm Bahamian blue under lashes as thick and shady as palm leaves.

"How about coming to dinner with me, Mel?"

Sometimes the register of his voice made her tingle like a tuning fork. How the hell did he do that? She meant to say no, but heard herself ask, "Tonight?" instead.

"Now," he said, opening her door. "Come on. I'm

famished. I thought I'd walk up to Papa Delgado's on Grant. Come with me."

"Well, I…"

"Come on. Lock up your car. Lock up your house. Let's go."

"I really hadn't planned…"

"I know," he said, and then reached into the car to pluck the keys from the ignition. "You don't have to plan everything, Mel. Some things just happen, darlin'."

That was precisely what she was afraid of.

Chapter 8

It was a lovely spring evening. In the park, the white dogwoods were turning a luscious pink as they soaked up the color of the sunset. Millions of leaves seemed to have popped open in the past twenty-four hours. The air had a touch of perfume in it. Sonny never noticed these details unless he was with Melanie. Without her, his environment was simply light or dark, hot or cold, wet or dry. Just one more reason he needed her, he thought. She civilized him.

And she needed him to add a little spontaneity to her rigid life, to make her laugh, not to mention returning missing spark plugs to her vehicle.

The worst of the rush-hour traffic was over now, but still Sonny linked his fingers protectively through Melanie's as they stood on the corner of Channing and Grant, waiting for the light to signal Walk.

Just as the light changed, a car sped through the intersection and squealed to a stop right in front of them. Well, calling it a car was an understatement. It was a two-tone, blue-and-white, heavy-on-the-chrome, convertible, pimp mobile. The license plate proclaimed Bigg Man, and that's just who appeared when the tinted window on the passenger door slid down. The big man. Elijah Biggs.

"You been hiding from me, Randle," he said, his lips sliding into a wide, oily smile.

Sonny shrugged. "Not well enough, I guess. You're blocking the intersection, Biggs."

"I'm looking for Lovey."

"Haven't seen her."

The pimp's gaze moved from Sonny to Melanie, paused for an appreciative moment, then returned. "Nice," he said. "Very nice. A little on the skinny side, though. Not much meat on those dainty white bones."

Sonny tightened his grip on Melanie's hand. The light changed and cars started honking.

"I'm going to write you up for obstructing traffic if you're not out of here in two seconds, Elijah."

The big man shivered, then smirked. "I'd sure hate that, Lieutenant. You see my Lovey, you tell her I'm looking for her. And you better tell her soon, you hear, or you'll be seeing me again. You know what I'm saying?"

The dark window glided back up. Biggs stepped on the gas and peeled away.

"Skinny," Melanie mumbled as she glared at the departing car. "Who was that?"

"Nobody," Sonny said, resenting the hell out of the fact that his job had once again encroached on his love life. His *real* life.

"Wasn't Lovey the woman you were talking to the other day outside Stover's?" she asked. "The one you wrote down your phone number for?"

He nodded.

"And now she's missing?"

He nodded again.

"Are you worried about that?"

It was Melanie who looked worried with her forehead crimped and her brows drawn together. The last thing he wanted was for her to be thinking about all the pimps, prostitutes and pure dregs of humanity he spent time with on the street. With his thumb and forefinger on her chin, he angled her frowning face up into his.

"Not tonight, babe. Tonight I'm worried about whether or not Papa Delgado's will have that red clam sauce you like so much. They didn't the last time we were there. Remember?"

Her gaze cut away from his for a second as if the memory were unwelcome, but then she laughed. "It wasn't red clam sauce. It was white. I remember the garlic."

Oh, yeah. So did he. When they'd made love later that night, she'd tasted like garlic. Everywhere. Ever since then, just walking into an Italian restaurant made him hard.

The light changed again. Sonny pulled her arm through his. "You're right. It was white. Let's go get some," he said.

Papa Delgado's was crowded for a Monday, and they had to sit at the densely packed bar for half an hour with their shoulders rubbing and their knees colliding before their table was ready. Melanie was having a really good time, but she kept telling herself she wasn't.

This was too much like when they were first dating, when Sonny focused his blue-green eyes on her to the exclusion of everything and everyone else, when he was sweet and charming and no doubt drugging her or putting her under some sort of wicked spell. She took another sip of her Chablis, swished it around in her mouth a second to see if she could detect something strange in its taste. Well, just because she couldn't taste it didn't mean it wasn't there.

He refused to talk about work. Instead he regaled her with stories of his partner Mike's TV-sitcom home life and the adventures of Baby Jacob, who seemed to consider both Legos and pocket change as edible.

"He swallowed coins?" Melanie gasped.

"Seventeen cents."

"Oh, my God." In all her fantasies about motherhood, she hadn't once imagined a kid who snacked on nickels and dimes. "What did Connie and Mike do?"

Sonny shrugged. "Just waited for it to come out.

Jakey only gave back sixteen of the seventeen cents, though.''

"How…?" And then it dawned on her. "Oh," she said, suppressing the *eeuuww.*

The maître d' signaled that their table was ready, and Melanie excused herself to make a trip to the ladies' room. While she washed her hands, she stared at her face in the mirror. Her eyes were bright, her cheeks were pleasantly flushed, and the corners of her mouth curled upward, giving the distinct impression of a happy person, which struck her as pretty outlandish since nothing had gone right since Friday afternoon.

She grimaced on purpose, then rummaged in her handbag for her lipstick, and while she dragged the color across her lips, she admitted to herself that she was still in love with Sonny. Who knew? Maybe she always would be. But that didn't alter the fact that she couldn't live with him.

"So don't look too happy," she warned her image in the mirror.

She found him at a table for two in a far corner of the back room, and then ignored his warm hand on her back when he stood to pull out her chair.

"I ordered for you, babe," he said, sitting down. "I hope you don't mind."

"Mind?" She could almost feel the furrows as they appeared across her forehead and the line that dug in between her brows. Her mouth tightened. "No, I don't mind."

Just after she spoke, the waiter slid a salad plate

onto the table in front of her. "House salad, madam, with the house vinaigrette on the side."

"Perfect. Thank you." Across the table, she caught the little glint of victory in Sonny's eyes. "Okay. So you paid more attention while we were together than I thought," she said a bit grudgingly.

"Give me a little credit, Mel."

She didn't want to. She knew him too well. Give Sonny Randle an inch and he'd go for a mile. Give him a little credit and he'd eventually break the bank. Or her heart.

He looked pretty smug all the way through the salad, and when their entrées arrived, Melanie knew why. He had ordered her the white clam sauce, but instead of the usual linguine, he had requested angel-hair pasta. Her preference.

"Thank you, Sonny. That was nice of you," she said without a trace of sarcasm.

"My pleasure, darlin'."

They were strolling home, and Sonny couldn't stop thinking about garlic. Crossing Grant, Melanie had slipped her arm through his and now her hip brushed against his with every step they took. Their conversation was easy and comfortable, devoid of sarcasm or bitter little zingers about their failed marriage. Mel was actually laughing. And he kept thinking about garlic.

Well, sex, actually. It had been so long since he'd had any that he might very well be confusing it with garlic, he thought. It wasn't that he hadn't looked at other women in the past year. He'd looked plenty. The minute word got out about his divorce, he'd been swamped with invitations for good home cooking, as if that was what he missed most about being married.

He'd looked, but he hadn't touched. Sometimes, when he let himself really think about it, which wasn't often, it scared the hell out of him wondering if he'd ever again want anyone but Melanie. Considering the depth of his need, it surprised him that he hadn't jumped her bones already on her sofa or in the front seat of her car or right here, right now, walking down the street.

Better just think about garlic, he warned himself.

"Do you think I am, Sonny?" Her question seemed to come out of nowhere.

"Do I think you're what?"

"A pill? A pain in the ass? Or…what was it you used to call me?"

"A picker of nits?" he suggested, trying to not laugh.

Much to his relief, Mel burst out laughing. She clung even tighter to his arm as her laugher dissipated to a series of sighs. "I guess I am. I don't know any other way to be. Details are important to me."

"I know that, babe," he said softly. "How could you grow up the way you did and *not* be a control freak?"

Her feet quit moving. Her arm jerked out of his. "I am not a control freak."

Oh, brother. He should have stayed with the garlic.

"Okay. Maybe that isn't quite what I meant," he said, backpedaling for all he was worth.

Her chin came up and her hands settled on her hips. "Well, just what did you mean, then?"

"I meant that you like your world to have a certain order."

"That's true," she murmured.

"Well. See. That's all I meant. Come on." He took her hand and started down the sidewalk again.

"Control freaks try to control others," she said. "I don't do that. Do I?"

He shook his head. This wasn't a good time to remind her that she'd spent her all her waking hours from age ten to age twenty-eight micro-managing her weirdo father, who apparently couldn't even go to the john without specific guidelines from his daughter.

"I'm not," she said again, even more vehemently, obviously unsatisfied by his silent response.

This time it was Sonny who halted. He turned her to face him, and then draped his forearms over her shoulders and bent his forehead to touch hers. "You're not a control freak, Mel. You're just highly organized. But, hey, if you ever do want to control somebody, look no further than me."

"You probably could use a keeper," she muttered grudgingly as garlic wafted up and hit Sonny's senses like a jolt from a cattle prod. He nearly staggered.

"Keep me," he whispered.

"What?"

Her head snapped up, and her wide eyes searched

his. For just a second he was seeing her though a fine mist, a wavering film that he quickly blinked away.

"I said 'Keep me.'" This time his voice was more or less under his control. "I really need you, Mel."

It was her voice that broke. "Oh, Sonny."

He couldn't prevent his fingers from sliding into her hair or his hands from angling her face for his kiss. She tasted like garlic and good wine and just plain Melanie. He deepened the kiss, needing to consume her completely, and she didn't resist.

At his back, a passing car honked.

"Go for it!" a voice yelled.

"You go, man!"

Sonny broke the kiss with a muted growl. "Come here." He pulled Melanie into a narrow walkway between two houses.

He couldn't think. He couldn't stop. Blood was hammering in his veins. In the darkness, he backed Melanie up against the side wall of the house, pinned her there with his weight, pressed into her warmth while he devoured her with kisses that she returned with equal fervor.

Like a kid on a hot date, he wrenched her blouse from her waistband and slid his hand along her ribs, up over the lacy fabric of her bra. It wasn't the gentle overture of a husband or even a randy date, but a headlong assault by a pirate who'd been at sea too long, a cowboy who'd been months out on the trail, a wild man who hadn't been with a woman in a year.

He was too rough. He knew it, but he couldn't help

himself. God. She tasted like sex itself. Her wet
mouth. Her sleek tongue.

"Sonny! Stop!"

He couldn't.

"Sonny!" she said more insistently, pushing at his
shoulders. "Stop! I mean it. Listen."

Then somewhere in the distance, with what was left
of his brain, he heard it.

A woman's voice crying out.

"Fire! Fire! Somebody help!"

They raced down Channing, already aware of a
sickening orange glow in the sky and flames shooting
from the upper windows of a house in the middle of
the block. The McKinleys? Melanie racked her brain
to remember who lived there. Not the McKinleys. It
was the Forresters. They had three little girls.

Sonny was holding her hand, but she realized she
was holding him back.

"Go," she told him, holding the stitch in her side
and gulping in air that already smelled like smoke.
"Hurry. I'll catch up."

Without her, Sonny was able to sprint much faster.
By the time she got to the house, he was nowhere to
be seen.

People were pouring out of houses all around the
square, some of them shouting as they ran toward the
burning house, some of them looking frightened and
dismayed in their approach.

"Did somebody call the fire department?" Melanie

asked a tall man in striped pajamas whom she didn't even recognize.

"Probably," he said. "But let's do it again." He pulled a cell phone from the pocket of his pajama top and punched the three-digit emergency number.

"Melanie!" Joan Carrollis grabbed her by the elbow. "This is just terrible. What if it spreads to the Dieffenbachs' house? The whole block could go up in flames. My God. What should we do?"

At this point, Melanie was far more worried about people than property. "Is everyone out of the house?"

Joan blinked. "I don't know."

Melanie listened for sirens and heard only the rush and crackle of the fire, the shouts of the crowd. There had been complaints at city hall about the department's slow response times. When she'd read "It took them eleven minutes" or "We waited a full fifteen minutes," the times hadn't made much of an impression on her. They did now. Each of them seemed like an eternity.

Suddenly, at the front door of the burning building, she saw Sonny talking to Bill Forrester, who was gesturing wildly toward the second floor.

"I'll be right back," she told Joan, then rushed toward the two men. Sonny was shrugging out of his jacket when she reached them.

"What's going on?" she asked.

"Emily's inside," Bill Forrester wailed. "She ran back to get her doll."

"Oh, God."

"Here, Mel." Sonny thrust his jacket at her, then wrenched off his shoulder holster and handed that to her, as well. "Hold these for me, will you? Don't put that weapon down anyplace. Just hold it."

"You're not going in there!" she exclaimed. "Sonny!"

He ignored her, turning to Bill Forrester to ask, "To the left or the right once I get up the stairs?"

"Left," the man replied. "Her room is the first door on the left."

"Sonny!"

"First door on the left," he repeated for Forrester's confirmation. "Okay. Got it."

"Sonny!" Melanie plucked at his sleeve, trying to get a grip on his arm.

"I'll be right back, babe. Better give me back my jacket. I might need it."

Rather than wait for her to hand it over, he pulled it from her grasp. Then, after brushing a quick kiss across the top of her head, he took the short flight of steps to the entrance in two leaps and pushed in the door. A thick haze of smoke immediately drifted out. And Sonny, with his jacket pressed to the lower half of his face, disappeared inside.

"Dear God, please let him find her," Bill Forrester said.

"He will." She gave his arm a reassuring touch. "I'm sure he will."

They both stood there staring at the smoke that was beginning now to roll faster and blacker through the open doorway. Melanie hugged Sonny's still-warm leather shoulder holster to her chest. She thought she was going to be sick.

Suddenly the sound of sirens blasted through the air and the ground almost shook with the approach of fire trucks and squad cars and ambulances. Brakes squealed. Doors slammed. Lights of every color cut back and forth across the Forresters' front lawn and all the people gathered there.

"You'll have to move back, sir. Lady."

The fireman who spoke was already gripping her arms, moving her brusquely aside, when Melanie said, "My husband's in there. He went in to try to find a little girl."

The man cursed and immediately yelled over his shoulder. "We've got civilians inside. Let's go. Let's go."

"He's not a civilian exactly," Melanie felt compelled to advise him. "He's a cop."

He cursed again, as if that were even worse than a mere civilian for some reason. "I just wish these hot dogs would quit thinking they can do our job."

Melanie had to bite her tongue to keep from saying "Well, somebody had to do it. You weren't exactly here, were you?"

Bill Forrester began to tug at the sleeve of the man's fireproof coat. "Hurry, please. My daughter, Emily, went back in for her doll. Upstairs. The second floor. The first door on the left."

Suddenly they were surrounded by half a dozen men, all looking huge in oversize black coats with yellow stripes, all of them gripping extinguishers or crowbars or axes.

"You'll have to move back, ma'am," a new arrival said. "You, too, sir. We'll…"

Melanie didn't move, but looked frantically at the front door just as Sonny staggered through it. "Wait. Look! There he is."

"He's got Emily!"

A spotlight from one of the patrol cars framed Sonny and the little girl in a circle of bright blue. It was an incredible sight, with little Emily clinging to Sonny's neck and his arms protectively surrounding her. Both of them were smudged with soot from head to toe so that the only bright spots on either of them were their eyes.

Emily's were huge and wet and dark in their circles of pale skin. Sonny's… My God. Even at that distance, Sonny's eyes were the endless and beautiful and beckoning aqua of the open sea. They nearly took Melanie's breath away. Then she stopped breathing entirely when she saw him close those eyes and press a gentle kiss to Emily's temple, when she read his lips telling the frightened child, "It's okay. It's okay."

Until that moment she'd never thought of Sonny as a father. Not once. A husband, yes. A mate. A lover, certainly. She'd thought of him as everything a man could be in this world except a gentle and protective father. Now the notion hit her with the force of a storm wave crashing on a beach.

Then she was pushed aside by firemen lugging

hoses and uniformed cops clearing the area. In the general melee that ensued, she didn't see Sonny again until she happened to glance at one of the ambulances. He was sitting on its rear bumper holding an oxygen mask over his nose. She elbowed her way through the crowd, and reached for the soot-streaked hand he held out to her.

"Hey, babe," he said, lowering the translucent mask.

"Are you okay?"

Before he could reply, a brawny female EMT who was standing nearby said, "He *says* he's okay, but I think he's a liar."

"Nobody asked you, Doctor Demento," Sonny growled in the woman's direction.

"*Are* you okay?" Melanie asked again, reaching out to touch his sooty hair. "Really?"

"I'm fine," he said. "Here, Doc." He handed the mask back to the scowling woman.

"Well, all right." She sighed gruffly. "But you go straight to the E.R. if you have any tightness or pain in your chest, okay? Or if you get short of breath." Her skeptical gaze slanted toward Melanie. "Are you his keeper?"

"Sort of."

"Well, smoke inhalation can be serious, so don't let him try to tough it out. Any wheezing, hoarseness, coughing, you get him to the emergency room on the double, you hear?"

Sonny stood and offered his hand to the paramedic. "Thanks, Doc."

"Yeah. Yeah. Go on. Get outta here," she said.

"I'll take my gun back now, Mel."

She'd completely forgotten that the holster was slung over her shoulder, the pistol tucked under her arm. Sonny slipped it off and eased it over his own shoulder.

"Where's your jacket?" Melanie asked.

"Trash can. That smoke will never come out of it."

They stood there a minute, looking at the commotion. The fire seemed to be under control, if not out entirely. The rolling black smoke had turned to rising gray steam. Onlookers were shaking hands, saying good-night, heading back to their own homes. As they passed, all of them called their thanks to Sonny or sent him a thumbs-up bravo for a job well done.

Sonny looped his arm around Melanie's shoulders.

"Let's go home," he said.

The night air smelled wet and acrid, all of its sweet spring perfumes covered over by smoke. Sonny was so quiet while they walked that she began to worry again about the effects of the smoke on him, but when she asked, he reassured her that he was fine.

"Why don't you come in and take a nice, hot shower?" she asked him when they reached her front door.

The invitation took Melanie completely by surprise. She hadn't planned to ask him. At least, she didn't think she did. It seemed to just tumble out of her mouth before her brain had given its final approval.

Too late to take it back, she told herself that her sole concern was Sonny's welfare. He was filthy—from his soot-coated hair to his singed shoes. He needed a shower desperately, and if there was water at all next door, it probably wasn't hot. She was merely being humane. A good neighbor.

Her offer had absolutely nothing to do with their gut-wrenching kiss earlier. She certainly wasn't picturing his lean and solid body in her steamy shower stall, all slick with soap and hot water streaming the length of him and swirling about his finely shaped toes before it disappeared down the drain. Why, that image had barely even occurred to her.

''Thanks, babe. But I think I'll just go next door and crash.'' He kissed her forehead. Just the lightest brush of his lips. ''Good night, Mel.''

And just as she'd denied that she wanted him to stay, now Melanie denied her disappointment that he was leaving.

''Okay,'' she said. ''Good night.''

Chapter 9

It was barely light the next morning when Sonny was awakened by loud, relentless banging on his front door. For a moment after he opened his eyes, he didn't even know where he was. Then his head solidified. Oh, yeah. The house from hell. And the knocking was Mike Kaczinski's familiar, big-knuckled, ham-fisted triple knock.

Knock, knock, knock.
Knock, Knock, Knock.

"Come on in. It's open," Sonny called, reminding himself once again to pick up a damn lock. He really needed to make a list, he thought, without the slightest trace of sarcasm.

Mike stood just inside the front door, balancing two large coffees in one hand and what Sonny hoped was a bag of glazed doughnuts in his other hand. "Morning, Fireman Fred," his partner said, not bothering to suppress a chuckle. "I heard about last night. In fact, I not only heard about, I read about it. You're on the front page of the paper this morning."

"Great," Sonny said sourly, taking one of the coffees and the paper sack from Mike and then continuing along the dark hallway toward the kitchen. "Remember in fifth grade when we were trying to decide whether to be firemen or cops?"

"Yeah."

"Well, we made the right decision, pal. That is one nasty occupation. I still can't smell anything but smoke."

Entering the kitchen, Mike gave a series of exaggerated sniffs while he glanced around the little room with its rust-stained sink and rotted linoleum. "Probably beats smelling anything else in here," he said.

"Still pretty much of a pit, huh?" Sonny shrugged helplessly, thumbed the plastic lid from his coffee cup and then blew on the steaming contents before taking a sip.

Mike nodded. He tried his own coffee, then said, "The word going around the shop this morning is that the arson guys found something suspicious down the street."

Sonny raised an eyebrow. "Like what?"

"Like an accelerant tossed through a busted back window."

"Oh, yeah?" He spoke as he dug through the half-dozen doughnuts in search of a glazed one. "Any idea why the family would have been a target for something like that?''

Mike shook his head. ''Nope. Not yet. They're going to talk to them today. But there's another theory going around I thought you might want to hear about.''

''Oh, yeah. What?''

''That the torch got the wrong house. That maybe he got the wrong street.''

Sonny dipped the doughnut into his cup, then bit off the soggy end. ''Meaning what?'' he mumbled, leaning back against the sink.

''Meaning the Forrester house doesn't look all that different from this one, Sonny. I just drove by the place. They're almost identical.''

''Well, almost. Except one's fairly decent and the other one's a real pit.''

''They're both pits now,'' Mike said. ''Similar street numbers, too. Theirs is 12024. Yours is 1224.''

He hadn't paid any attention last night to the appearance of the burning house or its address. ''Does this theory come with any names attached to it?''

''A couple,'' Mike said. ''Slink Kinnison. Elijah Biggs. Ring any bells?''

''Yeah. But not fire bells.''

''The Big Man is looking for you, Son. He has a bone to pick about one of his girls. You know who I mean?''

''Lovey,'' Sonny said. ''She hasn't turned up anyplace yet, has she? Has she contacted Heilig or White?''

"Nope. Not a word. Nobody's seen her on the street, either. At least not that I'm aware of." Mike glanced at his watch. "Gotta go, partner. You watch your back, okay?"

Sonny nodded. "Keep me posted, okay, Mikey?"

"Will do." He started for the door, then turned back. "Hey, how's it going with Melanie? Connie wants to know when you guys are coming to dinner."

"Soon," he answered without much conviction. "Soon."

After Mike left, Sonny polished off a couple more doughnuts as he gazed out the kitchen window. He turned Mike's information over in his head just once before tucking it away. He didn't want to think about the job. Not this morning.

Melanie had asked him in last night. If he'd accepted her invitation, he'd still be there this morning. He knew that as well as he knew his own name because he'd seen the heat in her eyes that had nothing to do with having just witnessed a fire.

It had been that body-slamming, heart-stopping kiss in the alleyway after dinner. The fire that kiss had started in him was comparable to the one in the house down the street. And Mel had caught fire, too. He'd tasted the flames.

Which was why he'd been a good boy, kept his gun in his holster, and gone home last night. He knew it was too soon for their bodies to reach the sweet accord that their minds hadn't yet agreed to.

This was too important to let unpremeditated sex get in the way.

This was his life.

What was left of it, anyway.

Melanie sat at her kitchen table, sipping coffee, attempting to read the paper but continually turning back to the front page to look at the picture from the night before. The photographer must have snapped it at the exact moment she was staring at Sonny and viewing him as a potential father.

In the photograph, just as she had witnessed last night, his eyes shone like soot-circled aquamarines. Little Emily's arms were flung around his neck, and his strong hands held her with such tenderness that she might have been a fragile porcelain doll rather than a flesh-and-blood little girl. His lips were just about to fashion the reassuring words that Melanie had seen him whisper to her. "It's okay. It's okay."

She refolded the newspaper, slapped it down on the table and set her coffee cup directly on top of the haunting, front-page picture, glad that at least somebody was okay because she certainly didn't feel that way herself.

She felt churlish, the best word she could come up with to describe her reaction to the wildly wavering emotions inside her. If she hadn't known precisely, almost to the minute, where she was in her monthly cycle, she might have blamed her mood on PMS, but that wasn't the case.

She loved Sonny Randle, but she couldn't live with him. Still, she didn't want anybody else to live with him, either. She wished he'd moved to the other side of the planet instead of the house next door, but at the same time she wished he were here inside *her* house. And not just in her house but in her bed.

She wanted him gone. She wanted him—period.

Her head felt as if it were going to explode from all the contradictory thoughts, and her heart was probably going to start fibrillating from all the crazy emotions there.

Everything had been fine until he'd moved next door. She'd missed him, but she'd coped with that while she got on with her life. Her plans for the baby had been honed to perfection, and now they were unraveling faster than a ball of yarn in a roomful of kittens.

Worst of all, Sonny—the man who almost prided himself on being lousy father material—was starting to look just the opposite. And in full color on the front page of the paper, no less!

It all just made her head hurt, and she was about to lower it into her hands when the object of her distress trotted down his back steps. His thumbs were hooked in the pockets of his jeans as he started a lean, loose-limbed walk down his driveway like a gorgeous guy who didn't have a problem in the world.

Melanie's immediate, knee-jerk reaction was to think, *He better not be heading over here,* even as her heart picked up speed in anticipation of. greeting him at her door. She sat at the table, ignoring her pulse rate, waiting for the inevitable chime of the doorbell.

Waiting.

And waiting.

Well, if he wasn't coming over to her house, where in the world was he going? She hustled into the living room to peek out one of the front windows, but she didn't see him anywhere. He was just gone.

Good.

Sort of.

Sonny stood on the sidewalk awhile, pondering the burned building that was now festooned with bright yellow police department tape. Mike was right. It did look a lot like his house with its rough, red sandstone bricks and tall, arched windows. The small front porches were similar, too, and but for the zero in the center of the numbers, their addresses were nearly the same. The Forresters lived at 12024 Channing while his house sat at 1224 Kassing. It would have been an easy mistake for a firebug to make, especially at night and if he were in a hurry, which of course he would have been.

Slipping under a line of yellow tape, Sonny walked around to the rear of the house. He called through what was left of the charred back door. "Hey! It's Randle, Third Precinct, Vice. Can I come in?" Most of the arson investigators in the city were prima donnas who tended to get squirrely if anybody walked unannounced onto one of their scenes.

"Hold on a sec. I'll come out," a voice grunted just before Eddie Zeile sucked in his gut and passed between the burned door and its blackened frame.

"How's it going, Randle?" The fireman stuck out a
meaty, soot-streaked hand.

"Fine," Sonny responded. "You find anything yet,
Eddie? Any idea who did this?"

"Yeah," he said. "An amateur with a glass jar of
kerosene and a pack of matches. Good help is hard
to find these days, huh, Sonny?"

Although he chuckled at the fireman's black hu-
mor, there was nothing funny about it. It was looking
more and more as if the fire at the Forresters' had
been a mistake. Still, there were more than a hundred
other houses in Channing Square to choose from.
Hell, maybe the dimwit firebug was supposed to torch
a place on Fanning Street halfway across town.

"Thanks, Eddie. If you could send an extra copy
of your report to me at the precinct, I'd appreciate
it."

"No problem. So you're the Cop on the Block?
How's that working out?"

"So far, so good," he answered, deciding there
was no sense telling him that in the four or five days
since he'd taken up residence there had been a rape
and a fire of suspicious origin. "Well, I'll let you get
back to work, Eddie. Thanks for the information."

"Take it easy, Sonny."

The fireman went back into the burned-out house
and Sonny continued on down the street, deliberately
avoiding a glance into the alleyway where he'd practically mauled Melanie the night before. He was really
going to have to keep a tight lid on that caveman stuff
from now on.

He turned down Grant, picked up his pace, and twenty minutes later was threading his way through a selection of minivans on the crowded tarmac of Howard "It's A Deal" Deal's used-car lot.

After a few bleak minutes of sticker shock and deep mourning for the Corvette, Sonny spotted just the vehicle he had in mind. A big blue box with a luggage rack on top and fake wood panels on the sides. A van that practically screamed "For the Family Man." By the time a salesman had hotfooted it out from the office, Sonny already had his checkbook in his hand.

Melanie stood in the nursery, a paintbrush in her right hand and the phone in her left. She was talking to Sam Venneman, or more precisely, she was talking to herself, having been put on hold for the third time while the mayor chatted up somebody else.

It had occurred to her earlier that, instead of spending all her time on an emotional roller coaster and peeking out windows like a crazy woman, she might just as well go back to work for the next few weeks. Not only would that preserve her sanity, but it would also guarantee a Sonny-free environment for eight or ten hours a day. That was why she had called Sam at city hall, but he'd put her on hold so often that she hadn't yet had a chance to mention coming back.

"Still there, Melanie?" Sam asked tentatively, as if he weren't sure he had pushed the right button.

"I'm here," she answered. "Sam, I was—"

"Wait just a minute, Melanie."

Even with his hand covering the mouthpiece, she

could hear a female voice in his vicinity while Sam murmured a string of okays and uh-huhs. Waiting for him to resume their conversation, she began picturing his calendar. Wasn't he supposed to be making a speech at a Rotary luncheon today? She glanced at her watch. He'd have to hurry to get there in time. Cleo Pierce wasn't doing her job if she didn't prod Sam away from his desk in a reasonable time to—

"Back again," he said cheerfully.

"Don't you have a Rotary luncheon today, Sam?"

"Do I?" He sounded surprised. "Wait. I'll ask Cleo." Then he covered the phone again for a moment. "Cleo said it was postponed until next week, Melanie."

"Oh. Well, if Cleo just came in to talk to you, maybe I should call back some other time."

"No. No. She didn't just come in. She's working temporarily at the coffee table here in my office because they're painting hers."

"Oh." Melanie frowned. The least he could have said was *yours*. "What color?"

"I have no idea," he said. "Wait. I'll ask her." There was more murmuring, and even some soft chuckling, before Sam said, "It's teal, Cleo says. More green than blue. What? Oh, more of a peacock green. She says she thinks you'll love it. Melanie? Still there?"

"I'm here," she said, trying to maintain a neutral tone similar to the one on the walls in her former office. Peacock green? She had a headache just contemplating it.

"Good," Sam said. "Sorry it's been so hectic here. I meant to tell you it was great seeing you and Sonny at the party Saturday. Did you watch the coverage on the eleven o'clock news?"

"No." Melanie rolled her eyes. "I missed it."

"Too bad. Thanks to Sonny, we scored a few nice points for the Cop on the Block program. Now what was it that you wanted to discuss with me?"

At this point Melanie had almost forgotten why she'd called him in the first place.

"Well, Sam, I was thinking…"

Her voice drifted off as her gaze strayed to the window. A blue minivan had just turned into Sonny's driveway.

"I was just wondering…"

The van pulled all the way to the back of the driveway as if intending to park there permanently.

"It occurred to me…"

The last person in the world she ever expected to see climb out from behind the wheel of a stodgy minivan was Sonny Randle, but there he was in all his long-legged glory. He stood there a moment, as if admiring the hulking vehicle, then slid open its side door, reached in, and pulled out a large brown grocery sack with a loaf of French bread sticking out the top.

"Melanie, you don't sound like yourself," Sam said on the other end of the line. "What's going on? Are you all right?"

"Well, Sam…"

A minivan? Sonny traded his Corvette for a minivan? He was now striding toward her house with an armload of groceries.

"I should probably go, Sam," she said. "Sorry I bothered you. I'll call back later when you have more time."

He was spluttering something very un-Samlike when she broke the connection.

A minivan? Groceries?

Melanie raced down the staircase and reached the front door at the same moment the bell chimed. Before she opened the door, she swallowed hard to clear her heart from her throat.

"Hey, babe." A grin blazed across Sonny's face. "I don't have a refrigerator yet so I was hoping I could stash some of this in yours."

She felt her mouth opening and closing without issuing any sounds. She probably looked like a goldfish that had just flopped out of its bowl, she thought.

Sonny cocked his head. "Is that a yes?"

"Oh, I guess so. Why not?" She stepped back to let him enter. The golden crust of the French bread passed inches from her nose, and her stomach growled in response.

"Hungry?" he asked over his shoulder as he started toward the kitchen.

Following behind him, she clasped her arms over her stomach to stifle the ridiculously loud noises. "No."

Sonny proceeded to empty the contents of the grocery bag on the kitchen table. First came the beautiful bread. Then lush red tomatoes. Carrots with long, leafy tops. A polished eggplant. A big, papery head of garlic. A box of imported pasta. A wedge of Parmesan. One surprise after another appeared from the depths of the sack until Melanie couldn't keep silent anymore.

"Who *are* you?" she exclaimed.

"What?"

"Who *are* you?" she repeated, gesturing toward the gourmet delights on the table. "Where's the Wonder bread? Where are the SpaghettiOs cans? The pretzels? Where's the six-pack of bargain beer?"

"I got this instead." He winked as he pulled a bottle of wine from the bag and perused its label. "Château Margaux '95. Think it's any good?"

"Good!" Melanie nearly choked. She didn't know all that much about wine, but instantly recognized the vintage that His Honor, the snob, had insisted they serve at his last inauguration dinner. The Bordeaux must've cost Sonny at least thirty dollars, she guessed. Maybe more. "It's better than good," she said. "Way too good to swill with your pals while you're tearing out linoleum."

"I thought we could have it for dinner."

"Dinner? When?"

"Tonight."

"I've already made plans." That those plans included frozen macaroni and cheese plus a can of warmed-up green beans wasn't something she felt obliged to disclose. "Go ahead and put whatever you want in the fridge. Here. I'll make room in the vegetable bin."

When Melanie opened the refrigerator door, the outpouring of cool air felt good on her face and neck. She didn't remember always feeling feverish when she and Sonny had lived together. Maybe she was actually coming down with something. It wouldn't have surprised her a bit, considering her level of stress and woeful lack of sleep these past few days.

She squatted, jerked open one of the drawers at the bottom of the appliance, then pushed aside a bag of carrots and some loose stalks of pale, limp celery. Stretching back her arm, she said, "There's plenty of room. Give me the carrots and the eggplant."

But instead of placing a vegetable in her open hand, Sonny grasped it with his own.

"Let's have dinner, Mel. Come on. You have to eat, right?"

Yes, dammit, she had to eat, but she wasn't sure she could even swallow the way her heart kept creeping up into her throat, not to mention her Sonny-induced fever. Now, all of a sudden, tears blurred her eyes, and she did her best to blink them away.

"Why are you doing this to me, Sonny?" The frustration she couldn't suppress any longer trembled in her voice.

"Hell, baby. I love you."

"Well, stop."

"I can't," he said softly as he knelt beside her in front of the open refrigerator. There was a rough, wet catch in his voice when he added, "I can't stop loving you, Mel."

"Oh, Sonny." She sighed and stared straight ahead

at the blurred picture of the missing child on the milk carton because she couldn't bear to look at her ex-husband. If there were tears in his beautiful eyes to match the sad sound of his voice, she wouldn't be able to restrain her own tears and she'd wind up in a soggy, salty heap right here on the floor.

"Let's start over, sweetheart." He slipped his arm around her shoulders and pulled her against him. "We could do that. Let's pretend we just met. We'll take it nice and slow and…"

"We didn't take it nice and slow when we met, Sonny," she said, knuckling a tear from her eye. "We didn't know how to do anything but hot and fast, and look where that got us."

He gave a mournful little laugh. "You're right. But it'll be different this time. *I'm* different."

"Maybe," she said with uncertainty. "People just don't change like that, though. God knows, I haven't changed."

"I don't want you to change, Mel. I want you just the way you are."

"Oh, please," she moaned, then leaned back far enough to close the refrigerator door with its burden of magnets, each of them holding up some sort of list. She gestured toward them. "Are you saying you really liked being married to Little Miss List Maker, the Queen of the Post-It notes?"

"I liked being married to *you,* babe. Not that I was around often enough to show it."

"You love your job, Sonny."

"Not as much as I love you. I guess it took that

bullet a couple weeks ago to get me to really see that.'' He sighed, tipping his head against hers. ''It scared the hell out of me, Mel. I honestly thought I'd been hit. I thought it was all over. I lay there on the pavement, thinking I was dying, maybe even already dead, and the only thing I regretted, the *only* thing, was not getting it right with you.''

''Sonny, it wasn't all your fault. I...''

''I want to do it right this time, Mel.'' His voice snagged again. ''Please.''

They sat there for the next few minutes without speaking. Above the low and continual hum of the refrigerator, Melanie could hear Sonny's deep and even breathing. His arm circled her shoulders, imparting his warmth, tempting her to lean against him just a little more while she considered all the reasons she ought to say no.

They were just too different. Day and night. Black and white. Sonny was a willy-nilly roller coaster and she was a flat, straight, well-marked road. Oil and water. Rain and shine. His weather was wild and unpredictable while hers was calm and carried the *Farmers' Almanac* stamp of approval. Dog and cat. High and low. The King of Chaos meets the Queen of Caution.

She had a million reasons to tell him no, not the least of which was that she simply couldn't endure the pain of another failure.

And yet, in spite of all those reasons, Melanie couldn't bring herself to say that simple word—no—because she had the feeling that if she said it, Sonny would never ask again. It would be more final than their divorce. She simply couldn't bear that.

"I… It's just that I had everything all planned out," she said, shaking her head, sounding so pitiful she could barely stand her own voice.

"I know."

"This house," she went on. "The nursery. The baby. The way Christmas will be a year and a half from now. Everything. But now it's all up in the air again."

"I know." His hand smoothed up and down her arm. "Don't answer right now, okay? Just tell me you'll think about it."

She lifted her hands helplessly, then let them drop back in her lap. As if she could think about anything else. As if she could think at all when Sonny was so close beside her.

"All right," she said. "I'll think about it."

"Good." Sonny sounded as relieved as she felt to have the situation temporarily solved. He stood up, and in one smooth motion lifted Melanie to her feet. "Now that we've got that settled, let's stash these groceries and go for a ride in my new van."

Chapter 10

The minivan handled like a Cracker Jack box mounted on four sticky licorice tires. It went from zero to sixty in about a month and cornered with all the precision of a rusty tricycle. Sonny hated it. But that was okay. He hadn't bought it to please himself. Melanie loved it, which was the whole point. As they wove through side streets to avoid the late-afternoon traffic, she kept smiling and looking back at the built-in child seat.

Sonny wasn't driving quite as aimlessly as it seemed. Mel wasn't the only one with plans, and right now his was to nail down this family-man image by stopping by the Kaczinskis' for a dose of unadulterated suburban bliss.

"This is Mike and Connie's street, isn't it?" she asked, squinting and pulling down the visor on her side to escape the bright late-afternoon sunshine.

"Yeah, it is. I thought we'd stop for a minute so I could give Mike a peek at my new wheels."

Even though his gaze held primarily on the street, he could tell Melanie was staring at him. She had shifted slightly sideways in the passenger seat. Her arms were crossed and her head cocked at a curious angle. Sometimes, because she was so predictable, he had an innate feel for what she was thinking. This wasn't one of those times, though.

"What?" he asked with another quick glance in her direction. She was wearing one of her most inscrutable smiles.

"I was just wondering," she said, "when you were going to 'fess up about missing the Corvette."

"I don't miss it," he lied, pretending to be shocked at the very notion.

"You loved that car, Sonny."

"Loved. Past tense, Mel."

"You had it for years. How many? Six or seven?"

"So?"

"Well, I just find it hard to believe that you don't miss it. That car was so…so *you.*"

"Was." He reached out to pat the dashboard. "This is me now. Solid. Steady."

"Square," she added with a laugh.

His mouth tightened and, for just a second, he was wounded by the description, until he reminded himself that square was good and precisely what he wanted to be. No more Joe Cool. He was Fred Family now. Harry Homeowner. Vincent Van.

But that new image suffered another blow when he turned the minivan into the Kaczinskis' driveway and

Connie came out of the front door trying to keep her eyeballs from bulging out of their sockets.

"I don't believe this," she exclaimed.

"See," Melanie said. "I rest my case."

Melanie had always liked Connie Kaczinski. The shapely blonde had been a photographer for Associated News, and had even been nominated for a Pulitzer prize, but had given it up when she'd given birth to Michael, Jr. six years ago. Now she took amazing photographs of birthday parties and backyard barbecues instead of three-alarm fires and scenes of brutal crimes.

The two women rarely spent any time alone. But now, while Sonny and Mike stood in the driveway nodding and rubbing their jaws as they did slow circles around the van, Melanie sat with Connie in the screened porch on the side of their house.

Connie had just moved the white wicker furniture out there today to take advantage of the warm spring temperatures. Six-year-old Michael was plopped on a floor cushion watching cartoons on a little TV, and Baby Jacob, taking a little breather from toddling, had kerplunked on the floor between the two women and was sorting plastic blocks by some secret system only he was privy to. Melanie could hardly take her eyes off the busy little guy.

"He really sold the Corvette, huh?" Connie said, tightening the blond ponytail at the nape of her neck and leaning back as if she'd had a long day. "I probably shouldn't tell you this, but I bet Mike twenty dollars that Sonny wouldn't be able to do it."

"That's okay. I would have bet twenty thousand dollars," Melanie said, stretching forward to pick up an errant yellow block for Jacob. "In fact, deep in my heart I still believe he's just got it stowed away in a garage somewhere close by so he can visit it every few days. Here you go, Jakey."

A pudgy hand grabbed the proffered block.

"What do you say, Jakey?" Connie said.

"Tanks," he said.

"You're welcome, kiddo. Wow. I can't believe he's walking and talking already, Connie," Melanie said. "I guess it's been almost a year since I last saw him."

The blonde frowned slightly in response, reminding Melanie that the Kaczinskis had been Sonny's friends for a long time before she was even a blip on his radar.

"Sonny looks happier than he has in a long time," Connie said. "It's none of our business, Melanie, but Mike loves Sonny like a brother. You know?" She turned her head to look at them out in the driveway. "Oh, jeez. Now they're looking under the hood like there's a pot of gold hidden in there."

Melanie turned to look. She probably shouldn't have. Sonny was reaching to fiddle with something near the engine, and the sight of her ex-husband's long, strong legs and the clearly defined muscles rippling across the back of his shirt made her mouth go a little dry. She could hear herself swallow, and wondered if Connie could hear it, too.

"Mike said Sonny went absolutely nuts when he found out you were planning to have a kid," Connie

said. "He put his fist through a door or a wall or
something at the precinct."

"That's not too hard to imagine." She sighed and
gazed down at little Jacob, who was licking a red
block as if it were a Popsicle. "Does that taste
good?" she asked him.

He held the wet block out to her. "Some?"

"No, thank you, Jakey."

"For what it's worth, Melanie, Mike thinks that
taking that bullet really changed Sonny. I wasn't quite
so convinced. I said I'd reserve judgment until he got
rid of the Corvette." She laughed. "I wonder if Mike
would consider taking that twenty bucks in trade."

As she was speaking, the two minivan inspectors
appeared in the doorway to the porch.

"You owe me twenty bucks," Mike said, winking
at his wife.

Connie laughed again. "I know. I know. How
would you like it? Two tens or a twenty?"

Mike waggled his eyebrows. "I'll get back to you
on that later."

Sonny seemed oblivious to the entire exchange.
Melanie watched him as he lowered himself onto the
sisal rug and settled next to the toddler. "How's that
thumb, Jakey?" He gently nudged the plump little
arm that was angled up toward a cherubic face. "Is
it pretty good?"

The little boy immediately plucked his pudgy, wet
thumb from his mouth and offered it to Sonny.
"Some?"

"No, thanks. I've got my own." He reached toward his back pocket, and, with a, *Ta-da!* produced his thumb.

Jacob whooped and chortled when the man beside him hunkered over and started sucking. "Mama, look Unca Summy!"

While Mike and Connie laughed, young Michael wandered over, his nose slightly out of joint at the attention being paid to his sibling, and threw his arms around Sonny's neck. Melanie watched as her ex-husband raised his free hand to clasp the boy's arm and remove his thumb long enough to quietly inquire, "How're you doin', partner?"

And then the oddest thing happened. While she sat watching him with his thumb in his mouth, with one little boy leaning on his knee and another draped around his neck, everything else in the world seemed to disappear. If Mike and Connie were still there, she was oblivious to them. It was as if she were suddenly looking through a narrow lens that focused solely on one man and two children. Or as if she were staring at a Norman Rockwell scene of a man who seemed utterly content, as warm as a hearth, as loving and dependable as any father ought to be. She longed to be in the picture.

Then, as she watched, Sonny slowly lifted his blue, shining gaze to meet hers, and something passed between them—something so intimate, so visceral, that Melanie could hardly breathe. If she hadn't already been sitting, she might have sunk to her knees. As it was, it was all she could do to remain upright in her wicker chair.

She wanted Sonny Randle that moment as she had never wanted him before. But more. She wanted...

God help her. This couldn't really be happening, could it? Was this how nervous breakdowns began, with tunnel visions of Norman Rockwell scenes? Had the King of Chaos finally driven her completely around the bend?

She wanted Sonny's child.

Was she nuts?

On the drive back to Channing Square, traffic was fairly light and Melanie was much too quiet. There was no ragging on him about the Corvette, no advice on whether to turn right or left, not even a single helpful murmur when a red light changed to green. She wasn't herself, except for when she pulled her planner from her handbag, made a quick notation, then put it away again.

Sonny started worrying that Connie might have said something while the two women were alone to make Mel feel sad or upset. Connie, after all, was on his side. She'd been even angrier than Mike when Melanie had ended their marriage after only six months.

They were just a few blocks from home when Melanie suddenly said, "We need to talk, Sonny."

His heart bashed against his ribs. He started to sweat. The last time he'd heard her say those words in that exact tone was when she'd told him she was filing for divorce.

We need to talk, Sonny. This just isn't going to work. I'm seeing a lawyer tomorrow.

Barely able to concentrate on the road, Sonny pulled over to the curb. He opened his window, sucked in a deep breath of air, then killed the engine.

"Let me go first," he said, trying to keep his voice on an even keel and his temper on ice when inside he was screaming, *You didn't even give me a chance, goddammit.*

He raked his fingers through his hair, wondering if Melanie would take pity on him if he cried, which was what he felt like doing. That, or ramming his fist through the dashboard.

"Did Connie say something to you earlier?" he roared. "Because if she did…"

"No. She didn't say a word. I just—"

"Okay. Wait. I want to go first here."

Sonny unsnapped his seat belt to shift around to face her. He draped an arm over the steering wheel, leaned back against the door a minute, closing his eyes, trying to get his thoughts in order because these might be the most important words he would ever speak in his life. He had to make Melanie understand not just how much he loved her, but how badly he needed her.

They'd spoken before about his childhood, but he had a tendency to make jokes about it and always glossed over the pain of being abandoned by his mother and then shunted from one foster family to another, each time having to learn new names, new rules, new everything, each time having to make his way through a new pecking order of kids who were usually angry at having to share a room or a parent's attention.

He didn't want to whine about the past. It was past, after all. Over and done with. He'd coped. He'd done the best he could for a kid who was forced through the revolving door of the system again and again.

Maybe, just as in his marriage, he'd done it all wrong with one foster family after another. But that didn't matter now. After all these years, he finally knew how to do it right. Especially with Melanie, his lovely list maker, the keeper of his chaotic heart. If only he could find the perfect words to tell her.

"Sonny," she said, putting her hand on his leg to get his attention.

He opened his eyes. "Okay. Just listen to me, will you? I know what I want to say to you, Mel."

"But, Sonny…"

He clenched his teeth. "Will you just wait until I've said what I need to? Please?"

More irritation sounded in his voice than he'd meant to convey, and he was just about to add an apology when Melanie interrupted him again, sounding pretty irritated herself.

"Well, okay. But it's going to be hard concentrating on whatever it is you have to say with that weird man standing behind you at the window."

"What?" Sonny jerked up, turned to his left, and very nearly touched noses with a man who looked like an extra in a werewolf movie.

A cheerful, "Hi, Lieutenant," wafted past Sonny's nose like a cloud of sewer gas.

"For crissake, Eagan." Sonny's startled heart slid back into its regular place. "What the hell do you think you're doing? You shouldn't sneak up on people like that."

"Oh, I'm sorry, Lieutenant. I thought you knew I was here and you were just ignoring me. People do that, you know. All the time. Ignore me. I'm used to it."

Sonny sighed. Carl Eagan was every cop's most pitied street person. The guy had lost half an arm and most of his mind in Vietnam. He'd been in and out of hospitals for decades, but no medication or treatment plan had been invented yet for his particular demons, whatever they were. Children shrank away from him. Cats and dogs even gave him a pretty wide berth. With wild black hair that shot out from his scalp and dripped from his upper lip and chin, he really did resemble a werewolf.

"I wasn't ignoring you, Carl." Sonny swore under his breath. "This just isn't a really good time to have a chat."

"Oh." The derelict's gaze wandered to Melanie on the passenger side of the van. He touched a nicotine-stained finger to the invisible brim of an invisible hat on his messed-up head. "Hello, ma'am. How are you?"

"I'm fine, thanks," Melanie answered in a voice that was unmistakably kind and sincere. She leaned across the center console, smiling. "How are you?"

"Oh." His yellowed fingers slipped inside his black beard for a quick scratch. "Not too bad. I've been better, I guess. I appreciate your asking. Most don't."

Sonny interrupted the love fest. "Eagan, this really

isn't a good time. Can I catch up with you tomorrow or later in the week?''

His werewolf face sort of crumpled underneath all the hair. Across the console, Melanie uttered a woeful little, ''Aw, Sonny'' as she put her hand on his arm.

''Give the poor thing a few minutes,'' she whispered. ''We're not in any hurry.''

No. Not anymore. Everything he'd been wanting to tell her had just fizzled in his brain. Right now, with Carl looming over his left shoulder, he wouldn't be able to persuade Melanie to take her next breath, much less marry him again and make him happy for the rest of his life.

''Okay, Carl.'' Sonny sighed. ''What's going on? Anything shaking out on the street?''

''I'm glad you asked, Lieutenant.'' There was no sarcasm in the guy's voice. His embattled mind had probably already erased Sonny's attempt just a moment ago to brush him off. ''People usually treat me like I'm stupid and don't know anything. But I do. I know things. I see things.''

''Like what?'' Sonny asked, hoping this wasn't going to be about little green men in space ships as was often the case.

''I know where Reva Edwards hid that grocery cart she stole from Kmart a couple days ago. I know ol' Dave Dellinger isn't cashing his own disability checks. And I know where Slink Kinnison is making his dope this week.''

''Whoa.'' Sonny sat up straighter. But as quickly as his cop antennae activated, so did his Melanie Meter. *Don't screw this up,* he warned himself. Do not screw this up. "I'm, uh, kind of on vacation, Carl."

"Cool," the man said. "Florida's always nice this time of year. I was there once."

"What I mean is…" Okay, he thought. He was still doing his job if he handed Eagan off to Heilig or White. Of course, he'd done that with Lovey and Heilig had just brushed her off because it was quitting time and God forbid he put in one minute he didn't get paid for. But what the hell. Sonny wasn't getting paid anything at the moment.

"I'm going to give you the name and number of a guy at the precinct," he said to Carl, then he asked Melanie, "Can I borrow a piece of paper and a pen?"

"No," she said.

"What?" He stared at her. Was she angry already? He hadn't even done anything. "What do you mean, no?"

"I mean no. Kinnison's your guy, Sonny. Why let Stan Heilig have all the fun?"

"Melanie." After he said her name, his mind went blank. In cartoons, characters always slapped the heel of a hand to their ear, just to make sure they'd heard correctly. Sonny felt like doing that now.

He didn't know what to say. To further complicate things, Carl poked his horrible head through the window and breathed through his mouth as he pondered the miracle of the dashboard.

"Uh, you want to step back just a bit, Carl? I need to have a few words in private with the lady."

"Oh. Sure. I can do that."

"Good. I appreciate it."

After he could breathe again, Sonny turned to Melanie. "I don't get it. You want me to follow up on this thing with Kinnison? I'm not even officially working, Mel." He stared at her harder. "And what do you mean, fun? You never thought this was any fun."

Her smile turned inscrutable again, a mysterious curve that Sonny couldn't begin to fathom, and she reached out to touch his cheek. "You're good at what you do, sweetie," she said softly. "Just be careful while you're doing it, okay?"

"You actually want me to go with Carl?" He'd never felt more stupid, more thickheaded. "This isn't some kind of trick, is it, where you'll beat me up later for taking off right in the middle of a discussion?"

The inscrutable smile turned sad. "I promise you it's not. We'll talk about it later, okay? Because I really do want to talk. How about if I whip something up from all those groceries you bought, and we'll have dinner whenever you're done with Carl and his information?"

"Sounds like a plan," he said, although what that plan might be was way beyond his ability to comprehend at the moment. If nothing else, they had a dinner date, and by then he might be able to prepare an impassioned speech to replace the one he'd just forgotten.

He turned to the window to see Carl Eagan, former marine captain, recipient of several Purple Hearts and a Silver Star that kept showing up in local pawn shops, standing on the sidewalk like a shaggy hitching post. "Hop in, Carl," he said, reaching back to slide the door open for the one-armed veteran.

"Oh. Okay. I'll do that." He clambered in awkwardly, then settled on the seat and looked around, sort of amazed and full of anticipation, as if he'd just taken a seat at the opera. "This is nice, Lieutenant. You should probably roll down the windows. I haven't had a shower in a while."

"That's okay, Carl," Sonny said. "You need help hooking up your seat belt?"

"Oh. Do I have to?"

"Yeah. You do."

Melanie, seemingly unfazed by the odor that permeated the vehicle, wedged between the front bucket seats and latched Carl in. "There you go," she said.

"Thank you, ma'am."

"You're welcome."

Sonny started the engine. "I'll drop you off at your place," he said to Melanie, "then take Carl to the precinct. It shouldn't take too long. An hour. Maybe two."

"That'll give me time to get dinner started," she said.

He thought about all the times he'd ruined dinners she'd spent hours planning and preparing. It wasn't a given that he'd be back in time for this one. The odds were good that he wouldn't be.

Before he put the van in drive, Sonny reached across the console for his ex-wife's hand. "I don't have to do this, Mel. Just say the word and…"

"Drive," she said with a little laugh. "We'll talk later."

*   *   *

An hour after Sonny had dropped her off, Melanie
stood in the kitchen, scraping carrots. If anyone had
told her a week ago that she'd be fixing dinner for
Sonny tonight—a dinner that might be served at eight
o'clock, or nine-thirty, or half past midnight for all
she knew, if it was even served at all—she would
have laughed out loud and then bet every cent in her
bank account that it would never happen.

Never.

Not in a million years.

But here she was, grinning like a complete fool,
peeling carrots, about to put together a red sauce and
let it simmer for however long it took for Sonny to
come home. It wasn't so different from the way she'd
felt two years ago when they'd first met, when the
King of Chaos kissed her for the first time, when the
Prince of Pandemonium played havoc with all her
plans and for a while, a wonderful while, set her free
from her burdens of caution and taking care.

My God, he'd done it again! He'd done it with a
single look. A look that found her heart with the precision of a heat-seeking missile and exploded any
plans she might have had that didn't include him.

It had to be drugs, she thought as she ground the
carrot peelings in the garbage disposal and finished
up the sauce in a blur of chopping, measuring, re-
measuring and stirring. Since she was already under
the influence, she opened Sonny's bottle of Château
Margaux, splashed a bit of the wine into the red
sauce, then poured herself a glass and carried it into

the living room where her father's stained-glass lamp cast its magic colors.

When she really thought about it, Sonny wasn't half as chaotic as her father had been. Sonny at least knew how to follow through with a plan once he'd begun, whether it was hunting down a drug dealer or pursuing his former wife. Pop, on the other hand, seemed unaware that there was any world at all outside of his artworks. He left all that to the women in his life—to her mother and then to Melanie. They'd both loved the man to pieces in spite of his carelessness and detachment. Who knew? Maybe they'd loved him because of it.

Maybe, in spite of all her protests, that was why she loved Sonny. He wasn't obsessed with crossing *t*'s and dotting *i*'s. God forbid she should find herself with a man who was exactly like her. They'd probably kill each other with perfectly sharpened pencils. Worse, they'd probably doom all their children to terrible tics and early nervous breakdowns.

She pictured Sonny again as he'd sat this afternoon on the Kaczinskis' screened-in porch, sucking his thumb, with Jakey at his knee and Michael clinging to his neck. She revisited that incredible look he had given her, the one that had melted her resistance along with her bones.

They could make this work, the two of them. She could make it work singlehandedly, if she had to, because this time she would know how to bend rather than break.

When the phone rang a few minutes later Melanie sensed immediately that her bending skills were about to be put to the test, and she had a pretty good idea what Sonny was going to say before the first apologetic word was out of his mouth.

"This is going to take longer than I thought, Mel."

"Okay." She took another sip of the mellow wine.

"The DEA guys are swarming all over this. They want to take down Kinnison's new place tonight, but…" He paused long enough to swear. "But it turns out Carl doesn't know the address. He says he'll know it when he sees it, but he won't go with these guys unless I go, too."

"Poor Carl. I can understand that."

Even as she spoke, Melanie could hear herself thinking, *Let's see… Dinner was simmering on the back burner, not to mention the simmering that was taking pace in several of her vital organs. She had plans for the evening that were unraveling. So, why wasn't she upset?*

"I'm sorry, babe. I know you're making dinner…"

"It'll keep," she said. "In fact, the longer it simmers, the better it will be."

He was quiet a second before he asked, "Are you okay, Mel?"

"Yes, I'm fine. Why?"

"You just sound…oh, I don't know…subdued or something."

"I'm bending, Sonny," she said, stifling a laugh. "Listen. You take care of Carl and get home when you can. Use the key under the *W* in the Welcome mat."

He sounded as if he were only half joking then when he asked, "You're not going to be behind the door with a rolling pin or a cast-iron skillet in your hand, are you?''

''No.'' She laughed. ''As a matter of fact, I'll probably be in bed, which is where I hope you'll be joining me sometime before dawn.''

She actually heard him swallow. It was nice, once in a while, to be able to flabbergast the King of Chaos.

''Let's make a baby, Sonny,'' she said.

He swallowed again, louder. ''Mel, I... Aw, dammit. They're getting ready to...'' Away from the phone he called, ''Yeah. Okay. Okay. I'm on it.''

Then he was back, his voice low and sensual. ''Are you sure about this, Mel?''

''I'm sure.''

''Under the *W* in Welcome, huh?''

''Yes,'' she said, smiling. ''Hurry.''

''Oh, yeah, babe.''

Chapter 11

It was nearly three in the morning when Sonny got back to Channing Square. In spite of all the open windows, the minivan still smelled like Carl. Sonny'd even run the air conditioner full-blast in the hope that it would push out some of the foul odors, but no such luck.

They hadn't had much luck with the bust tonight, either. Everybody and his brother wanted in on it— the DEA, the Marshals, the Feebs—so that by the time a couple gallons of coffee were consumed and the chain of command was finally hammered out, Carl was so confused he barely knew where he was, much less where to locate Kinnison's new meth lab. Eventually Carl recognized the place on Third Avenue, but it turned out to be merely *a* meth lab, not necessarily Kinnison's.

Then, since nobody volunteered to see their fragrant informant back to his refrigerator box, Sonny had taken him through a drive-thru for a couple of burgers before letting him out at his current address, the Bristol Avenue overpass.

After he parked the van at the back of his house, he briefly considered checking on the place like a responsible property owner, then decided he'd much rather check out Melanie's house where the front light was still burning bright. He trotted up her front steps and looked down at the carpeted mat beneath his feet.

W, he thought, didn't just stand for Welcome. It also stood for Wonder, which was what he'd been doing most of the night. Wondering what had made her change her mind. *W* stood for Wine, too, and he wondered if the hint of liquid he'd detected in her voice was responsible for her sudden randiness and the unexpected invitation into her bed.

Last, but hardly least, *W* stood for Wallet. He slid it from his back pocket, opened it, and checked under the leather flap to make sure the condom he'd carried for the past year hadn't disappeared or disintegrated. With a sigh of relief, he saw that it was still there, although he wasn't sure about its condition. Hell, he hadn't carried one of these for a whole year since he was a hopeful and highly motivated sixteen-year-old.

After he slipped his wallet back into his pocket, he squatted to search for Melanie's key, which turned out to be wedged between layers of the mat. In his capacity as Cop on the Block, he was going to have to tell her to start leaving a spare key with a neighbor, preferably him, instead of a dead-giveaway spot like this.

He turned the key in the lock, then quietly walked inside. The smell of spaghetti sauce immediately hit his senses and made his mouth water, but it wasn't a late dinner that was on his mind.

Melanie was sound asleep upon the sofa in the living room, with one arm crooked beneath her head and the other curled against her chest. The oversize T-shirt she wore rode high on her hip, revealing a lovely length of thigh. Sonny just stood there, loving her, enjoying the view.

He was glad to see she still slept in those silly shirts. It was such an un-Melanie thing to do. She was really more the silk-and-satin type. Anything she did that went against her precise, perfect grain always pleased him for some reason. It might have been because her loving him, a lowly cop, had always struck Sonny as such an un-Melanie thing when she could have had her pick of slick attorneys, camera-friendly journalists, or any number of hot-shot politicians.

It wasn't easy to drag his gaze away to go to the kitchen to turn off the low heat under the pot on the stove, then to check the back door to make certain it was locked before he took her up to bed.

"Hey, baby," he whispered, brushing his lips across her ear. "Time for bed."

She smiled without opening her eyes. "Mmm. You're home."

He slid his hands under her shoulders, beneath her knees. "Here we go. Put your arms around my neck."

She did, sighing and clinging to him like a little girl who couldn't bear to wake from a sweet, sweet dream.

He negotiated the staircase gingerly, only to realize at the top that he didn't know which room was Mel's. A small lamp burned on a table in the second-floor hallway. He chose the door to the left of that, using his foot to push it open, and knew immediately he'd made the correct choice. It was Mel's room, all right, with the bed made up with military precision but nearly sagging beneath a couple dozen pillows. Big ones. Little ones. Square. Round. Heart-shaped. Needlepoint. Petit point. Cross-stitch. He'd forgotten half the things they were.

He remembered, though, that going to bed was always a damned production, first fighting the pillow collection and then having to contend with the tightly tucked-in sheets. As much as he'd grumbled about it when they were married, he wanted to laugh now. He'd missed everything about Melanie, including her stupid pillows.

This time, though, Sonny didn't bother sweeping the pillows onto the floor. He lay Melanie down in the center of them. While her arms still clung around his neck, he was tempted to taste the sweet wine-scented lips that were just inches from his face, but he knew once he started he wouldn't be able to stop. Or worse, because it had been so long since he'd last loved her, that he'd go the distance from start to finish in thirty seconds flat, which wouldn't exactly be an idyllic beginning to their second time around. And even worse than that was the fact that, without a decent shower in days, he probably smelled an awful lot like Carl right now.

He brushed his lips softly against hers. "I'm going to take a shower, babe. I'll be right back."

"Mmm," she murmured, her eyes still closed.

Sonny reached up and gently loosened her grip on his neck. He found the bathroom easily enough, and after he flipped the lights on, he caught himself smiling in the mirror as he surveyed the items decorating the white marble top of the vanity. A place for everything and everything in its place.

The soap dispenser sat just to the left of the hot-water faucet. Perfume bottles convened on the right atop a little mirrored tray, each label facing exactly the same way. In front of the fragrances, Melanie's comb and brush lay side by side, about an inch apart. Always the same distance between them. The little bathroom in his loft had been arranged identically when she'd lived there.

He remembered, during those six brief months of marriage, how he used to twit Mel by turning one or two bottles of her cologne the opposite way every time he left the bathroom, and how they'd always be back, facing the front like good little soldiers, whenever he returned. Or how he'd always playfully plant her comb crossways, deep in the bristles of her hairbrush, and then come back a short time later to find them once more neatly side by side.

God, how he'd missed her bone-deep sense of order. Right now, seeing all these objects in their proper spots only made him want her more.

He reached into the shower stall to turn on the water, and while he waited for it to heat, decided it would probably be a good idea to brush his teeth. Knowing Melanie as well as he did, he knew there would be at least six spare toothbrushes lurking somewhere, perfectly aligned in their unopened boxes.

Glancing at the drawers on the left side of the vanity, he pondered a possible location. Let's see. If he knew his girl the way he thought he did, they wouldn't be in the top drawer, whose space would be reserved for items used on a daily basis. And they wouldn't be in the larger bottom drawer where she'd keep only oversize things that didn't fit elsewhere, such as bottles of mouthwash and shampoo and cream rinse. That left drawers two and three.

On a hunch, he reached down and pulled the third drawer open. There, among spare disposable razors, extra bars of soap and tubes of toothpaste, and next to a little white bale of cotton pads, were half a dozen brand-new toothbrushes. Ha! He plucked out a blue one and shucked off the cellophane wrapper, which he obediently tossed in the tidy little wicker trash can.

Steam from the shower was already coating the mirror over the sink, so while he brushed his teeth Sonny couldn't discern the worried lines etched across his forehead. Melanie wanted a baby. And not just any baby now, but his. Once again he pondered the question that had been gnawing at him all evening long. Mel wanted his baby, but did she really want him, too?

The longer he thought about it, the more hesitant he became to start something—namely a child—that Melanie wasn't going to let him finish. She'd walked out on him once. What would prevent her from walking out again, only this time taking his son or his daughter with her? He wanted to make damned sure that *she* was damned sure before that little boy or girl became anything more than the current gleam in his eye or the ache in his groin.

When he finished brushing his teeth, he looked around for a good place to put his toothbrush, then finally decided to play it safe by stowing it in his shirt pocket so he didn't disrupt the symmetry of Melanie's countertop.

Then, with a sigh, he shrugged out of his clothes, left them in a pile on the floor, and stepped into the billowing steam of the shower.

Nestled all snug in the pillows on her bed, Melanie listened to the rattle and moaning of the ancient pipes deep within the walls of her house. Sonny had just turned on the shower. It would be another five minutes, though, before he stepped under the cascading water. He'd brush his teeth, or shave, or put in eyedrops, do anything to dawdle while he waited to see if the hot water was going to turn ice cold.

The delay was one of his few idiosyncrasies, one he'd acquired during all those years of being shunted from one house to another, from one unknown plumb-

ing system to another. It was more than just a preference for steaming hot showers. It was as if he'd
decided early on that the world itself was cold and
unpredictable enough without constantly risking the
disappointment of hot water turning lukewarm on its
way to freezing cold.

That's why he ate fast, too, without even being
aware of it. Not that he'd ever actually told her, but
Melanie knew from several heart-to-hearts with Mike
that Sonny had gone to bed hungry more than a few
nights in elementary school and junior high. One family in particular had made him wait until their natural
children had eaten before the "foster boy" was fed,
and then the mother, for lack of a better term, had
always grabbed his plate before he was done because
she wanted to finish cleaning up the kitchen.

She sighed and sank deeper into the pillows. It
made sense. Her own childhood experiences were still
dictating her behavior to this very day. Why would it
be any different with Sonny? As a child, she'd had
to keep everything in order to make certain her world
didn't collapse, to keep from losing her father the way
she'd lost her mother. Sonny had to eat fast before
his plate was snatched away and he had to test the
water to make sure it would stay hot.

What a pair! They were poster children for the notion that opposites attract. They were probably perfect
mates with Sonny proving to her over and over that
the sky wouldn't fall if she failed to make a list or to
arrange everything just so, and with her proving to

him that life could be beautifully predictable and utterly reliable.

Well…except she hadn't really done that, had she?

My God! Melanie jerked upright, spilling pillows onto the floor on both sides of the bed. She hadn't shown him that life could be predictable or reliable at all. What she'd done was walk out on Sonny, proving to him once more that nothing was reliable, that he shouldn't depend on anyone but himself. In all the months since their divorce, Melanie had never looked at it as anything but her own escape from his chaotic lifestyle. Not once had she considered it from his point of view, so it had truly never dawned on her that she was abandoning Sonny the same way his mother had, the same way all those foster families had.

How could she have been so selfish? How could she have been so ignorant, so blind to the possible damage her leaving might do to him? How could Sonny even consider taking a chance again after what she'd done to him?

All she wanted to do just then was to throw herself in his arms and ask him to forgive her, and at the same time to throw her arms around him and tell him she'd never hurt him again, never leave him again.

Unable to wait, Melanie scooted off the bed and headed for the bathroom where she could still hear the water running in the shower. When she opened the door, it took a moment for her eyes to adjust to the steamy atmosphere. Sonny's clothes were in a jumbled pile on the floor, and she had to battle her impulse to pick them up and neatly fold them. She must really be a sicko, she thought, if the urge to tidy up was almost as powerful as the urge to join her naked ex-husband in the shower.

She could see him through the wavy, wet glass of the shower stall, the details of his powerful body just a flesh-colored blur, but even so her heart beat a little faster and an urgent warmth she hadn't felt in a long, long time reverberated deep inside her.

''Sonny.'' She called his name softly, but he didn't hear her over the sound of the cascading water. She started to speak again, but just then came the sound of a cell phone buzzing somewhere in the pile of Sonny's discarded clothes.

No. No way. Not now. Sorry. This was one time she wasn't going to let his job or anything else come between them. There would be plenty of emergencies and interrupting calls in the future, hundreds of them, and she vowed that she wouldn't complain about a single one of them. But not this one. Not tonight.

Melanie bent down, fumbled until she found the little black phone tucked in the back pocket of Sonny's jeans, and pressed a button to put it out of commission.

Then, without any hesitation, without even bothering to take off her big T-shirt, she opened the glass door of the shower stall and stepped inside.

Sonny nearly jumped out of his skin.

He'd been standing with his eyes closed, nearly comatose under the pulsing stream of hot water while it pounded out some of the tight knots in his neck and shoulders. Then, all of a sudden, he felt a quick current of cool air on his back. He pivoted, and there was Mel with her hair getting wet and her pink T-shirt starting to mold itself to her lush, wonderful breasts. He didn't even have time to let out a surprised curse before she plastered herself against him and turned her pretty face up toward his for a kiss.

Ah, God. He'd actually been standing here thinking how Melanie would probably be fast asleep when he finally dried off and joined her on the pillowy bed, thinking how he'd almost be relieved that they'd be able to postpone making love until they'd come to an understanding about the future, about the two of them, or the three of them if that was going to happen.

But here she was, her wet arms winding around him, her wet mouth beckoning his. All of Sonny's good intentions shattered from the force of the explosion of his need.

A kind of whimper broke in his throat as he lowered his head to take possession of her mouth. At the same time his hands moved, one to curve around her neck, the other up beneath the wet cotton of her shirt. He'd barely sampled her mouth, though, before he was dragging the drenched shirt over her head and then kissing his way from her delicate shoulders and collarbone down to the fullness of her breasts.

Somewhere in the soggy recesses of his brain a little voice cautioned Sonny to be smart, to take it slow. But he wasn't smart. He was on fire. He couldn't take it slow. He no longer knew the meaning of the word. And neither, it seemed, did Mel.

With her wet mouth at his ear, she pleaded, ''Now. Oh, God, Sonny. Please. Now.''

With his hands hooked under her arms, he lifted her enough for her legs to circle his hips.

''Hang on, baby,'' he whispered as he slid his hands around to cup her backside, getting a firm grip, and then eased inside her as gently as he could considering the almost diamond hardness of his erection and the fierceness of his need.

If her soft moan was from pleasure or pain, he didn't know. He couldn't even think anymore. Only feel. Only give himself over to pulsing water and rising steam and wet flesh and the heat ripping through him.

Melanie, too. For every thrust, she begged for more, harder, faster, until Sonny's vision blurred and there was nothing in the world but white light and water and the rocketing hot pleasure of their climax.

Her legs were trembling when he lowered her. Still holding her against him, Sonny turned off the water. He opened the glass door and snagged a towel.

''Are you okay, babe?'' He tilted her chin up and gazed into her eyes. ''Mel?''

She let her breath out in a shaky sigh. Her lips were slightly swollen, but they managed to twitch into a smile. ''Was it always like that?''

''Not always,'' he said with a little laugh. ''If it had been, I think we'd both be dead by now.''

''Or burned to a crisp.''

"That, too." He smoothed his thumb across her mouth. "What a way to go, though, huh?"

He wrapped her in the big soft bath towel and carried her back to bed.

Melanie awoke an hour or so later and smiled. Just smiled like a simpleton. A sated simpleton. There was nothing in all creation to compare with the radiant heat of a naked man in bed.

She stretched, almost perversely enjoying the dull ache in her thigh muscles and lower back. Reaching her hand across the several inches of mattress that separated them, she ran her palm lightly along Sonny's arm and shoulder, relishing the feel of his skin and the tough musculature just beneath it. She listened to the cadence of his breathing, not even caring if that tiny rough catch turned into a full-fledged snore.

Good Lord, she must really have it bad, she thought, if Sonny's snoring was suddenly the music of the angels.

Once again, she tested the various parts of her body that ached or felt tender. It wasn't so much that she was out of shape, but just that it had been so long since she'd had such explosive sex. If ever.

She smiled again in the darkness and was about to let herself drift back to sleep when it suddenly occurred to her to wonder if she was pregnant. All she'd thought about earlier during the mind-blowing, toe-curling sex, if she'd thought of anything at all, was the mind-blowing, toe-curling sex itself. She remembered what Peg had said on her last day at city hall, about insemination by the genuine article as opposed to the artificial means.

Her smile widened perceptibly as she reached out to touch Sonny again, and she fell asleep thinking that the real thing was definitely the way to go.

Chapter 12

Early the next morning, Melanie was still smiling as she moved around the kitchen fixing breakfast. Unlike most mornings, though, she kept getting distracted.

The first time happened when she was making coffee. She'd forgotten how many scoops she'd already measured into the basket, so she'd had to dump it all back into the canister and begin again, not bothering to level off the excess in each scoopful because she knew that Sonny liked his coffee strong.

Then, while she was taking eggs from the refrigerator, she started thinking about the baby again. She'd chosen the names Alex and Alexis based on her maiden name, Sears. Now that the baby's surname would be Randle, she wanted to reconsider those first names. Plus, Sonny might have one or two definite opinions about a name.

Also, she decided, she really ought to keep a record of their lovemaking to help her pin down the exact moment of conception.

Back went the egg carton. Out came a pen to make a small notation on the calendar she kept on the refrigerator door.

After that she couldn't stop herself from peeking ahead nine months on the calendar, and then she peeked farther ahead, to December, picturing the baby's first Christmas. But this time Sonny's handsome face played a major role in her recurrent mother-and-child fantasy. Now she envisioned three red-and-green stockings hanging from the mantel, and for a moment she could actually see her husband's strong hands with the fingers slightly splayed to cradle a tiny person in a tiny pair of bright red Christmas jammies.

Well, except he wasn't her husband. Not yet.

She should probably be looking at the month of June and fantasizing about a wedding. It was only when she heard the water running upstairs that she suddenly realized she'd been daydreaming so long she'd completely forgotten to pour water into the coffeemaker, not to mention the eggs and everything else about breakfast.

So Melanie, the Princess of Planning, the Paragon of Preparedness, suddenly found herself scrambling around the kitchen to get the coffee brewing and the eggs scrambled before Sonny came downstairs. She almost laughed at her own distractedness and lack of efficiency, wondering if it was even possible to be wildly in love and minimally efficient at the same time, trying to recall if she'd been quite this ditzy the first time around.

It took Sonny a bit longer to come downstairs than Melanie had anticipated, and she was sitting at the table, halfway through her first cup of milk-diluted coffee and a revised list of baby names, when he finally appeared in the doorway.

As soon as she looked up and saw him standing there—jeans riding low on his lean hips, no shirt to disguise the sculpture of his chest, no shoes, bleary blue eyes and a day's worth of rough whiskers shadowing his jaw—Melanie wanted him. Wanted him with a vengeance. She absolutely ached to feel Sonny inside her again, and it had nothing whatsoever to do with creating a baby. She wanted him just for herself. Right here. Right now.

For the first time she noticed the bruise on his chest where she assumed the Kevlar vest had stopped the bullet during the drug raid. The knowledge that she'd almost lost him before they'd had a chance to try again only increased her present desire.

Melanie took a quick sip of her coffee, hoping to clear her heart from her throat and maybe douse a few of the flames kicking up inside her. She'd consider herself lucky if steam didn't start escaping from her ears and nose.

"Morning', darlin'," Sonny said in a voice that was still a bit roughened by deep sleep.

"Good morning," she replied cheerfully, enormously relieved that the words didn't come out of her mouth as vapor instead of sound.

Out of a corner of her eye, she watched Sonny amble across the kitchen toward the coffeepot, and was immediately struck by the subtle change in his demeanor. He didn't move like a guest in her house anymore. He seemed perfectly at ease, reaching into a cupboard for a mug as if he knew just where it would be and filling it with dark liquid from the pot. As he sipped, he wandered over to the refrigerator where he stood staring at the calendar fastened to the door.

"What's the *F* for, Mel?" he asked between sips.

When she'd made the notation of their lovemaking, she'd chosen an obvious initial from the four-letter word she was sure she wouldn't confuse with anything else. It also stood for fertility. She had debated using I for intercourse, but decided she might confuse it with the Roman numeral one, and *S*—for sex—was already taken to signify shopping.

"It's for us last night," she said. "I'm really serious about this baby, Sonny."

"Yeah. I can see that." He kept staring at the calendar. "If you weren't serious, you wouldn't have used a capital *F*."

Melanie put her pen down on top of her baby name list and pushed her chair back. "It's just a way of keeping track."

"Ah. So the *F* is for…"

"Fabulous," she murmured, sliding her arms

around his waist and pressing her cheek to the warm skin of his back. "Fantastic."

"Well, that's a relief, Felix." He let out an exaggerated sigh. "For a minute there I thought it was a grade."

Melanie laughed softly. "No. I don't post those on the fridge. I keep them in my secret notebook."

"I see," he said. He drained his mug, then reached out to set it on the counter before turning to pull her close against him. "So," he whispered, "what did I get?"

She loved the feel of his lips drifting across her temple, warming her with his breath, stoking the fire inside her. "Last night?"

"Uh-huh."

"You got an *A*-minus."

Sonny jerked his head back and glowered down at her. "An *A*-minus?" he muttered. "An *A-minus?*"

It was all Melanie could do to not burst out laughing. She did her best to keep a straight face. "Well, there has to be room for improvement, don't you think, if we're going to be doing this for the next fifty or sixty years?" As she spoke, she pressed her hips against his.

"Well, yeah, but…" Sonny's words diminished to mere breath as he kissed her ear, her jaw, her neck, her collarbone.

Trying to pretend she wasn't tantalized one bit by the kisses, Melanie murmured, "It makes perfect sense. See, if I had given you an *A*-plus for last night, Sonny, there wouldn't be anything left to strive for or to look forward to." Her hands were moving over the lithe muscles of his lower back, along the waistband of his jeans. Her fingers were nearly tingling with his heat.

"That's true." He stopped kissing her long enough to lift his arm, crook his elbow, and cast a lazy glance at his watch. "Kinda early for striving, Mel. It's seven-fifteen."

"Mmm," she purred. "I've been looking forward to striving since I woke up at six."

She slid her fingertips into his back pockets, intending to urge him even closer. Her right hand encountered his cell phone in one pocket just as her left came into contact with a little square package that felt suspiciously familiar.

"You won't be needing this," she said, easing the wrapped condom from its snug place against his backside. "Might as well just pitch it," she added breezily. "What do you think?"

Sonny didn't say a word. He stood motionless, not even trailing those delicious kisses along her throat anymore.

What had she done? Melanie wondered. Had she made him angry somehow? She didn't understand this at all. It was pretty unnerving, being kissed and fondled one minute, and getting the silent treatment the next.

"What?" she asked.

"Mel." He sighed, then looked down at the floor for a second—pretty guiltily, Melanie thought—before he said, "We need to talk."

"About what?"

"This." He took the little package from her hand. "And that." Now he angled his head toward the calendar.

Her heart started drumming, this time with absolute dread instead of wild anticipation. She felt a little dizzy. A lot dizzy. "I think I need to sit down."

While Mel sat stiffly, as if she'd just been strapped into the electric chair, Sonny poured himself a second mug of strong coffee. He had to be the world's biggest jerk for doing what he'd just done, telling a woman in obvious heat that it was time for a little talk.

"More coffee, babe?" he asked.

"No. No, thank you." Her voice wafted across the space between them like a chilly breeze, but even so there was the smallest suggestion of a tremor in it.

God. What did she think he was going to say to her? Better yet, what the hell *was* he going to say?

You hurt me, Melanie?

You broke my heart?

Broke his freaking heart! What kind of geeky, whiney, adolescent sentiment was that?

He strode across the floor, thumped his mug of coffee on the table, turned one of her bentwood chairs around and straddled it. It wasn't so different from the routine he went through before he questioned a suspect. Brusque. Intimidating. He could feel his adrenaline kicking up.

You broke my heart.

You might as well have stuck a knife in my gut.
You hurt me.

"Look, Mel, I just think we ought to…"

There weren't any more words to be had, not safe ones anyway, not ones that could make it past the lump gathering in his throat, so his mouth just hung open for a moment before he snapped it closed and shook his head. "I don't know," he muttered. "Hell."

"Well, I don't understand this," she said in a tight, small voice. Her fingers were trembling as she fiddled with the pen and pad of paper on the table in front of her. She'd already rearranged the salt and pepper shakers half a dozen ways, and aligned her mug of coffee so its handle sat on a perfect east-west axis. "I thought… Don't you want to have a baby, Sonny? Is that what this is all about?"

"Yeah," he murmured. "Sort of."

Her gaze jerked up from the notepad. There was surprise, disappointment, even a little despair in her expression.

"No," he said quickly, trying to erase that wounded look. "That's not what I meant. I'd love to have a kid. I just don't think we should rush, that's all."

"'Rush'?" She repeated the word as if she didn't quite comprehend it.

"I think we should wait until we're sure," he said. "About us."

Then, still unable to get to his own painful bottom line, to articulate his deep hurt, Sonny let his voice drift off again. God, he was such a coward. "I think we should take it slow. Just to make sure. Take some precautions. You know."

She sat up a little straighter and her blue eyes got a little frosty. Her voice iced over when she said, "I noticed you weren't in a rush to take any precautions last night."

"You ambushed me." A little grin flared, then fizzled on his lips.

Across the table, however, Melanie wasn't grinning. Her lips turned down in a bitter curve. To Sonny, his ex-wife looked as if she'd been sucking on lemons for the past year or so.

"Oh," she exclaimed. "So it was all my fault, then?"

"Last night wasn't anybody's fault, Mel, for crissake." His hands came up and his voice rose in spite of his intention to keep it level and low. "Will you just listen to me for a second?"

Before she could reply, the doorbell rang. They both sat quietly, glaring at each other—a featherweight and a welterweight, sent to their separate corners by the bell.

Without a word, icy or otherwise, Melanie pushed back her chair and stood. She cinched the sash of her robe with such force she nearly bisected herself at the waist, then squared her shoulders and marched out of the room.

Melanie probably wouldn't have been so quick to open the door if she hadn't been angry or if she hadn't been aware that she was reasonably safe with the Cop on the Block just a shout away. When she jerked the door open, Sonny's partner, Mike Kaczinski was just reaching for the buzzer again.

"Hey, Melanie," he said, giving her a quick, tight smile. "I'm sorry if I woke you up. I know it's really early, but I figured… Well, I was looking for…"

His glance flicked over her shoulder, into the hallway. "There you are. I've been trying to call you for hours, man," Mike said irritably. "I guess you turned your phone off."

"What's up?"

Sonny's deep voice reverberated through Melanie's bones as he came up close behind her. She could feel his body heat seeping through the fabric of her robe. For a moment she forgot that she was angry and bitterly disappointed, forgot that he was still the same old, haphazard, not-ready-for-fatherhood man she'd once been married to.

"A body in a Dumpster," Mike said. "It wasn't easy to identify it, but we're pretty sure it's Lovey."

Now Mike glanced at Melanie again, and she instantly read the meaning of his all-too-familiar expression. It was a combination of *Pardon me, little lady, I don't want to burn your delicate ears* and *Sorry, ma'am, but this is official police business.* It was a look that had irritated her in the past, but right now she was more than happy to take the hint.

"Well, I'll just let you two have some privacy."

She ducked beneath the arm that Sonny had braced against the door frame and beat a retreat to the kitchen. Once there, she plopped back into her chair at the table and stared out the window while she absently listened to the low and serious ''cop'' voices filtering back from the front door.

Her gaze played over the house next door. The house. The thirty-year mortgage that went with it. The stupid minivan parked in the drive. What was all that? Just a way for Sonny to worm his way into her house and eventually into her bed, and then, once there, letting her know he really hadn't changed at all? Was it all a ploy to get back at her for being the one to leave?

If so, she'd fallen for it like a ton of used Channing Square bricks. Like a willing fool. All that remained to be said now was one big *Gotcha* from Sonny.

She heard his footsteps going up the stairs and a moment later caught a glimpse of Mike strolling around outside the house next door. He gazed up at the boarded windows on the second floor and shook his head in a kind of bafflement, then sauntered over to the huge Dumpster, stood on tiptoe, and peered in. It was the cop in him, she thought. Sonny did the same thing. Wherever they were, they were always on the lookout for dead bodies.

She felt like one herself at the moment, a corpse sitting at the kitchen table, one who simply hadn't had the good sense to fall over yet.

''I've got to go down to the precinct for a while, Mel.''

Sonny was standing in the doorway, tucking his white polo shirt into his jeans. He'd already slipped on his shoulder holster, along with his stony-cop expression. All he lacked was a big shiny badge pinned to his chest, a bright tin star that proclaimed *Sheriff*.

"Fine," she said, hearing her cold tone and hating the way she sounded. The word came out of her mouth like an ice cube from a dispenser.

So, of course, Sonny offered one of his beleaguered sighs as he came toward her. "I wish I had time to fight, babe," he said, leaning to kiss the top of her head.

For Melanie, all of a sudden it was déjà vu. It was their marriage breaking apart, shattering all over again. It was almost too much to bear a second time around.

"Mel?" He tilted her chin up.

"What?" *Plink*. Another ice cube.

"I love you."

Then it wasn't ice cubes falling from her mouth, but hot tears streaming from her eyes. She couldn't even speak except to utter a choked, "Oh, Sonny," as he strode out of the room.

Mike was wearing dark shades on the drive to the station so Sonny couldn't read the look in his eyes, but there was no mistaking the grin that kept flitting across his partner's lips.

"Say it," Sonny said from the passenger seat of the unmarked Mercury.

"What?"

"Whatever it is that's putting that goofball smirk on your face."

The goofball smirk turned into a laugh. Mike took

his left hand off the steering wheel and cupped it to his ear. "Listen, Son. Do you hear that?"

Sonny rolled his window down a few inches. "I don't hear anything but traffic."

"Oh. Okay. Never mind." Mike gripped the wheel again. "I thought I heard the tinkling little sound of wedding bells."

"Very funny," Sonny grumbled.

"So, do I need to get my blue suit to the cleaner's so I can play best man again?"

He didn't answer, partly because he didn't know the freaking answer, and partly because he didn't want to think about Melanie right now. Every time he thought about her, he saw those huge tears running down her cheeks. And what had he done about them? Pretty much the same as always. He'd walked away as fast as his fumbling feet would carry him. God. He'd rather take on six drugged-up, knife-wielding, jack-booted gang members than one tiny, crying woman. Mel didn't cry often, but when she did, it killed him. It just killed him.

"Tell me more about Lovey," he said, reaching into the pocket of his windbreaker for a cigarette.

"I told you all we know so far," Mike said. "A couple sanitation guys found her body late yesterday behind a Dumpster they only pick up once a week. The medical examiner estimates she's been dead four or five days. The official report should be coming in sometime today."

Sonny cupped his hand around the lighter's flame,

pulled in a long drag, then blew the smoke out the window.

''I thought you were trying to quit,'' Mike said.

''I am.'' He exhaled more smoke along with a muted curse. He thought of Saturday night when he'd scoured half the city looking for the prostitute after her frightened phone call. Lovey was probably dead even before he'd given up and gone home.

Whoever had beaten and stabbed her, had also stuffed the piece of paper with Sonny's address and phone number in Lovey's mouth. Only it turned out that Sonny, rushing to join Mel, had scribbled the wrong numbers for the address of his new house. He'd written the numbers of the house that had been torched the other night.

Slink Kinnison's message was abundantly clear. Anyone who snitched on him could expect the same treatment that Lovey had received. And Sonny, as the ringmaster of those snitches, better back off. Or else.

Sonny swore again. ''Goddamn that Heilig. This wouldn't have happened if he'd done his damned job right, if he hadn't cared more about dragging his ass home the other night than he cared about giving Lovey some protection after she begged him.''

''Hey.'' Mike's voice was sterner than usual. ''Heilig's got two-year-old twins and a brand-new baby in an incubator at Saint Catherine's. Cut the poor guy a little slack on this one, okay?''

''Yeah. Yeah. Okay,'' Sonny muttered.

''That could be you in a year or so, partner, if Mel gets what she wants.''

Sonny took a last harsh drag on his cigarette, then flicked it out the window before he said sourly, "Mel doesn't know what the hell she wants."

"I want a stage, Dieter. I want a real, working stage with a fancy proscenium arch and rich blue-velvet curtains that really open and close. The whole deal. And I don't care how much it costs." Melanie gave a shrug and then softened her tone a bit. "Well…you know…within reason."

Dieter Weist had shown up unexpectedly this morning at the tail end of Melanie's crying jag. One look at her red-rimmed, swollen eyes and he'd apologized profusely, offering to come back some other time to give her an estimate on construction in the playroom. But she'd insisted he come in. Maybe she was falling apart, but she'd be damned if all her plans would, too. And the more Sonny *didn't* want a baby, dammit, the more she *did*.

The beefy German nodded solemnly now and proceeded to pace off the east wall of the third-floor playroom, carefully planting one sturdy brown shoe in front of the other.

"Twenty feet all together," he said when he reached the southern end. "We could construct a platform sixteen feet wide and leave a twenty-four-inch access on each side. What depth were you imagining, *liebchen?* Maybe six feet? Eight?"

Melanie frowned. She hadn't even considered the depth of the stage, and it irritated her that she'd overlooked something so important. "What do you think?'' she asked the architect. ''Six feet doesn't sound like enough.''

She tried to picture children in costumes—pirates with plywood swords, fairy godmothers waving glittering magic wands, and angels with big cardboard wings.

He paced off six feet from the east wall. ''Here,'' he said, and then he took two more steps and spread his arms wide. ''Or here. This is eight feet.''

''There,'' she said. ''That's good. Right where you are now.''

Looking from where Dieter stood toward the rest of the playroom, she decided the stage wouldn't encroach too much on the rest of the space. There would still be ample room for all the wonderful things she'd put on her playroom list, for the toy chests and the easels and a play kitchen and a little make-believe grocery store.

''*Zehr gut.* Well, let me make a few little notes here and a preliminary sketch.'' He pulled a small black notebook from his pocket and began to write.

''Would you like a cup of coffee, Dieter?''

''*Ja.* That would be nice, Melanie. Don't go to any trouble, though, for me.''

''No trouble at all,'' she said, heading downstairs to the nearly full pot of the strong brew she'd made for Sonny a few hours before.

Let's see. One wasted pot of coffee today. One way-overcooked pot of red sauce yesterday. As far as she could see, things were pretty much back to normal as far as she and Sonny were concerned. The status was pretty quo. Chaos reigned once more.

In the kitchen it occurred to her, as she reached for a mug in an overhead cabinet, that she wasn't doing a very good job of bending the way she'd told Sonny she would do. But then, as she filled the mug with the hot dark liquid, Melanie decided that wasn't exactly true.

She didn't care about the wasted coffee or the ruined red sauce. They didn't really matter at all. What mattered was that she was thirty-one years old and ready, eager, determined to start a family, and that Sonny, the man she loved with all her heart, was not. It was as simple and as devastating as that.

"We'll talk about it later," he had said.

What was the use?

Dieter called down from the third floor. "Come up here, Melanie. I have a wonderful idea for a storage area underneath the stage."

Good. She carried Dieter's coffee up the stairs. If this storage area turned out to be big enough, maybe that's where she'd put all her useless plans and dreams about having Sonny's baby.

Chapter 13

Sonny sat at his desk in the big squad room of the precinct, feeling useless and frustrated and mad as hell. It had been almost two weeks since he'd been on vacation, long enough for somebody to mess up his Rolodex, break his stapler, and completely rearrange his personal stuff on the desktop.

Melanie's picture in its little silver frame—the one he'd taken of her outside city hall on their wedding day—had been shoved behind a stack of files and phone books. He pulled it out, ran his thumb gently over her pretty face, then stowed it carefully in a side drawer. Right now he wasn't sure if that photograph wasn't all he'd have of her for the next half century.

He closed his eyes a moment and clenched his teeth, trying to drive away the painful doubt.

Dammit. He needed to work.

But the captain had made it clear—mostly by hammering his fist on his blotter—that Sonny was still on personal leave and therefore forbidden to investigate Lovey's death in any official capacity whatsoever. He'd used the word "whatsoever" about a hundred times, trying to get his point across.

"Look, Randle," Captain Callahan had said between whatsoevers and beats of his big fist on his desktop. "We all know it was Kinnison, okay? We're on it. I've got four people out there right now, looking to tie him to that Lovey woman, as well as the arson in Channing Square. I know you think this is some kind of personal vendetta with Kinnison, and I appreciate that. It very well may be. Hell, it probably is. But you are not to get involved with this in any way whatsoever. Not until you're back from leave. Do I make myself clear?"

Callahan went on to remind Sonny that the police board would be convening next week to review the shooting incident at the meth lab, and it would be extremely unfortunate, a damned shame in fact, if a certain vice lieutenant's personnel file contained a fresh reprimand from his immediate superior.

Reprimand me for *this,* Sonny thought as he opened the center drawer of the desk and bashed it closed as loud and with as much force as he could, not once, but twice. *Blam. Blam.* A stack of files fell over onto the floor, but not a single person in the squad room even turned around to look. Outbreaks of violent temper involving kicked desks, ripped papers, shouted curses and slammed-down phones were a pretty normal occurrence around here on both sides of the law.

A few minutes later Mike signaled to him from across the room.

"What's going on?" Sonny asked, joining his partner in the hallway.

"Sorry I brought you in for nothing, Son. I really thought Callahan would make an exception in this case."

"Yeah. Well, no such luck." Sonny tried not to grumble and gripe too much. It wasn't Mikey's fault, after all. "Hey, it's okay. Really. What's one more week? Hell, I can use all the leave time I can get to work on that wreck of a house." *And the wreck of a relationship,* he added to himself.

"You need a ride home?"

"That'd be great, Mikey. Thanks."

Together, they started down the hallway toward the elevator. They had only taken a few steps when Stan Heilig came out of an interrogation room. As the lanky, blond detective approached them, Sonny's first instinct was to offer a sarcastic, teeth-bared thanks for all of his help with Lovey.

But when he heard Mike mutter, "Take it easy, Son," he found himself thinking about what Mike had said earlier about Heilig's new baby in an incubator in the hospital, and suddenly—feeling a kind of empathy with the guy—Sonny heard himself saying almost pleasantly, "Hey, Heilig. How's it going? How's the kid?"

Stan Heilig blinked as he grasped Sonny's extended hand There was more than a little wariness in his expression. In fact, he seemed to be tensing in anticipation of a blow. "Hey, Randle. She's better. Thanks. I just got off the phone with my wife. She's bringing the baby home today."

"Great news," Mike said, giving the young man a thumbs-up.

"Glad to hear it," Sonny said.

The tall detective still seemed on his guard. "Are you, uh, are you back on the active roster now? I thought…"

"Next week," Sonny told him. "See you then."

"Right. Okay. I'll see you. Take care, Sonny."

Heilig proceeded down the hallway toward the squad room, glancing over his shoulder as if to reassure himself he wasn't being stalked.

"That wasn't so bad, was it?" Mike grinned as he punched the elevator button.

"Must be tough," Sonny said quietly, "having to spend so much time with scumbags when all you want is to be watching over your sick kid."

After they stepped into the empty elevator, Mike pressed the button for the first floor, then said, "So this reunion with Melanie… Is it going to happen?"

Sonny stared at the procession of lit numbers on the control panel in front of him. He'd managed to forget about his ex-wife for about six minutes. Now her tearful face reappeared before him and his doubts came back. He shrugged helplessly.

"I don't know, Mikey. I'm beginning to think this

isn't going to work. Mel just wants a baby. She's obsessed with the idea. She doesn't really want me.''

Mike did his own version of a shrug while he stared at their blurred reflections in the polished doors. ''Why can't she want both?''

The elevator bell dinged to announce their arrival on the first floor. The door slid open, and Sonny, frowning, followed his partner out.

''What did you say, Mike?'' Whatever it had been, the words had caused something to click in Sonny's brain.

''I said there's no law I know of that says Melanie can't want both of you. You *and* a kid. It's not a mutually exclusive deal, you know.''

''Right,'' Sonny murmured.

He considered his friend's words as he followed Mike along the corridor to the back door and out to the parking lot. Maybe he had been thinking about this all wrong. Maybe Mel wanted him for more than a warm alternative to artificial insemination. Maybe he was just as important to her as a kid. Maybe this time she wouldn't pick up her ball and go home.

''Hey, Lieutenant!''

Sonny turned to see Patrolman Tim Moore loping up behind him. The kid was in street clothes and he looked as though he needed some sleep. Even so, he wore a kind of goofy grin on his face.

''Just getting off duty, Moore?'' he asked.

''Yeah. Finally. I always really look forward to walking out the door and catching my first glimpse of the mean machine.'' He pointed far across the parking lot where the sleek and shiny black Corvette was parked, far away from other vehicles.

"Not taking any chances on dings and dents, are you, kid?" Mike said with a laugh.

"No way," the young man exclaimed, grinning and jingling a set of keys as he picked up his pace and walked past them. "Hey, I don't even like anybody breathing on her."

"Sonny was always the same way," Mike said, "at least until he joined the minivan set."

The patrolman stopped and shook his head as if he couldn't comprehend how any sane man could even be tempted to give up a vintage Corvette in favor of a suburban special. "Do you miss her, Lieutenant?" he asked.

"Her?"

"Well, I call it 'her,'" Moore said almost sheepishly. "My wife's not too crazy about that."

"I guess not," Mike murmured.

"So, any regrets, Lieutenant? Do you miss her?"

"Nah."

As soon as the word came out of his mouth, Sonny realized just how much he meant it. He gazed across the lot at the car, fully appreciating its sleek lines and air of imminent danger, but failing to experience even a tiny pang of regret. He didn't miss the Corvette a bit. Melanie was all he missed, and he couldn't wait to get home to tell her so.

If he'd had any lingering doubts at all about his intentions, they were all gone now. This wasn't an act. The house. The mortgage. The minivan. He was playing for keeps.

"I don't miss her a bit," Sonny called out. "Take good care of her, Moore."

The patrolman waved over his shoulder as he continued to the far end of the lot.

Giving Sonny a little shot with his elbow, Mike said, "I'd say the kid's almost as crazy about that car as you are."

"As I *was*," Sonny said, correcting him.

"Oh, yeah. Sorry. I forgot."

They walked the last few yards to Mike's unmarked car. It had rained while they were inside, but now the sun was trying to break through the gray clouds overhead. Sonny took that as a hopeful sign that Melanie's wet weather had changed, too. They'd take a walk in the sunshine in Channing Park later. They'd talk this all out, and then get on with their life together. They'd make a baby, maybe even today, and the kid would simply cement the bond that already existed between them.

Really anxious to get back to Channing Square now, Sonny walked around to the passenger side of Mike's car, but just as he reached for the handle, a huge explosion ripped through the air, slamming him hard against the door as glass and metal and bits of leather rained down from above.

With his ears still ringing from the explosion, he barely heard Mike exclaim, "My God, Sonny. Oh, my God. That was the Corvette. That was meant for you."

* * *

After Dieter left, Melanie was sorely tempted to sink back into the funk she'd been in earlier, but she decided that would only be surrendering to Sonny's effect on her and his ability to swing her moods wildly from one direction to another. She'd choose her own mood, thank you very much, and—dammit—she was going to resume her own cautious and carefully plotted course.

Sonny may have thrown her for a loop with all his talk of how he'd changed, but she was back on track now. For a little while she had thought she could have it all—both Sonny and a baby. But it was pretty clear that her ex-husband didn't want a child any more now than he had when they were married. Fine. Okay. She'd just get on with her own itinerary.

The good news was she had plenty to clean and tidy up what with Sonny's presence in the house lately. She started with the bedroom where the sheets and blanket bore witness to who had slept on which side of the bed the night before. The covers on her side were neatly peeled back, giving her just enough room to exit, while those on Sonny's side were completely untucked and frightfully scrambled, as if a tornado had spent the night on that half of the mattress.

Melanie rolled her eyes and made a disdainful little cluck with her tongue, but at the same time she could feel her throat thickening and moisture building in her eyes. Ah, God. She'd taken a huge step forward this past year only to have Lieutenant Flummox send her reeling three or four steps back.

All she wanted to do right now was to sit on the bed and weep, but she fought down the urge with a vengeance, kicking strewn pillows out of her way and then ripping the covers from the mattress as if she meant to tear them all into shreds. Then, while she was pulling fresh sheets and pillowcases from the linen closet in the hallway, she thought she heard a car door slam at the curb out front.

If that was Sonny, she was ready for him and for their postponed talk. She was going to tell him that their separate visions of a future together were far too different to allow either one of them to be happy. It didn't matter that they loved each other if they couldn't agree on having a family. It was over. Period. It was time for them to stop pretending that there was any hope at all.

As she trotted down the stairs, the doorbell began to ring rather insistently.

"I'm coming," she called.

He wouldn't be in such a damned hurry, she thought, if he knew the bad news awaiting him once she opened the door. When she did open it, however, it wasn't Sonny standing there with a sexy grin on his face but Sam Venneman, who was wearing such a somber, almost-funereal expression that his normally tanned face appeared nearly white. Melanie could only gasp.

"Oh, my God, Sam! What's wrong?"

"There's been an explosion, Melanie. A car bomb, they tell me, in the Third Precinct parking lot."

"Oh, my God!"

Her knees began to liquefy and questions started ricocheting inside her head. Had Mike and Sonny gone to the precinct? How long ago was that? Or had they gone someplace else entirely? Why was Sam here telling her this?

"What…?" She could barely make her lips move. "Who…?"

"It was Sonny's car," Sam said, reaching out to grasp her arm. "I'm so very sorry, Melanie."

"No." The word came out calmly enough, although it sounded hollow and empty of emotion. It held no shock. No pain. Nothing at all. To Melanie, the sound seemed to come from someone else, someone far away.

She had gone completely numb from her head to her feet. Sam's face registered a sympathy she refused to accept. He'd just told her… What? Something that didn't make sense somehow, but she couldn't process it or get the information to fit with other scattered bits of knowledge in her brain.

"No," she said again. She sounded like a zombie, but she couldn't help it.

This was all wrong. Sam was standing there all tense and on the verge of tears as if he'd just relayed the news that Sonny was dead. But that was impossible. The sun was shining now. The park across the street looked beautiful in its spring colors. Melanie herself was breathing. None of which could possibly be happening if Sonny, the love of her life, were dead.

"Where is he?" she asked, not quite so calmly now.

"At the precinct," Sam said. "Let's go in and sit for a minute, shall we? Maybe you should…"

"No. Take me there, Sam." She stepped forward, forcing the mayor to take a step back, pulling her front door closed behind her. "Take me there right now."

"Do you want to get your handbag first? Your keys? You really ought to lock up."

"It doesn't matter." The whole place could burn down or disintegrate behind her for all she cared just then. Nothing mattered but Sonny. "Take me there right now."

She started walking toward the mayor's long black limousine that was waiting at the curb. All of a sudden a squad car came roaring around the corner of Kassing Avenue and slid to a stop in front of the limo. The car's flashing lights made Melanie dizzy, and her vision kept narrowing, as if she were going to faint.

"Get in, Melanie," the mayor said. "I'm going to see what these officers want."

She sat in the back seat of the limo, staring blankly out the tinted window. Something just didn't fit. It was something about the car. It was something about Sonny's car, but she couldn't get it straight.

The squad car, its lights flashing and its siren blipping at intersections, escorted them to the Third Precinct headquarters. Emergency vehicles and television news trucks blocked the streets around the three-story building, but the mayor's limousine was guided summarily through the tangle of vehicles and finally coasted to a stop directly in front of headquarters.

"I don't know how long we'll be here, Henry," Sam Venneman said to his driver.

"That's no problem, boss. I'll wait right here." The barrel-chested chauffeur extended a gray-gloved hand to assist Melanie from the rear of the limo. "I'm sure sorry about your husband, Miss Melanie. He was a fine man."

As she slid from the back seat, Melanie merely murmured, "Thank you, Henry," for the condolences rather than explain to the man that it was impossible for Sonny to be dead because... Because... Well, if for no other reason, then because she simply wouldn't permit it.

Sam grasped her arm and began to lead her toward the front door of the building. He used his free arm to wave away the oncoming horde of journalists with their extended microphones and Minicams.

"Can you give us a few words, Mayor?"

"Have they told you the identity of the victim yet, Sam?"

"We're hearing it was Lieutenant Sonny Randle, Mayor? Can you confirm that?"

"Melanie, can we get a quick statement? How do you feel? What have they told you?"

The mayor moved a protective arm around Melanie's shoulders and pressed relentlessly through the crowd. "No comment," he said again and again. "No comment."

It occurred to Melanie all of a sudden that this was

the first time Sam Venneman had ever told members of the press to buzz off. In all the time she'd known him and worked closely with him, Sam had never refused to take advantage of any sort of emergency— no matter how gory or grim—to get his pretty face on TV screens all over the city and his pearls of wisdom printed in the newspaper.

Melanie started shaking. My God. If Sam was behaving like this, so out of character for him, then this nightmare might be real. Maybe it was true. Maybe Sonny *was* dead.

No. No. No. She absolutely refused to allow that thought to take up residence in her head. If she didn't think it, then it couldn't possibly be true.

Her knees were feeling liquid and loose, her heart was pounding, and she was starting to hyperventilate by the time they went through the front door of the building with the press still on their heels. Without Sam to steady her, she might have crumpled to the floor. The mayor was apparently leading her toward the elevator when Melanie caught sight of Mike Kaczinski standing in front of a rest room door.

"Wait, Sam. There's Mike," she said, pulling her escort in that direction.

As they approached Mike across the precinct's lobby, Melanie got the impression that Sonny's friend and partner was standing guard in front of the rest room door. She distinctly heard him say to someone, "This one's out of order. Sorry. You'll have to use the rest room on the second floor."

"Mike," she called as she got nearer. "Mike. Oh, my God. What's going on? Where's Sonny?"

"Melanie! I'm glad the patrolmen could find you to bring you in right away," he said, then added a quiet, "Hi, Your Honor" in acknowledgment of Sam.

"Sam brought me," she said. "Where's Sonny?" Melanie could barely control her voice. "Where is he? I want to see him right this second. Now. Sam seems to think that... I won't let him be dead, Mike. I just won't. I won't."

"Whoa. Slow down, kiddo." Mike reached out to wrap an arm around her, tugging her closer to him to whisper in her ear. "Sonny's in here. In the men's room, Mel. That's why he sent the guys in the squad car instead of coming himself. He just needed to be alone for a couple minutes."

"He's all right, then! He's alive! Oh, thank God," she cried.

"Wait just a moment," Sam said, edging closer. The three of them must have looked like a trio of conspirators. "I was informed that Sonny's Corvette was blown up in the parking lot this morning. Are you saying that's incorrect?"

"Yes, sir. It was his vehicle. Well, his former vehicle, actually. But Sonny wasn't in it. It was Patrolman Timothy Moore, but we're withholding his name pending family notification, sir."

"I see." The mayor's tense mouth relaxed a bit and his pallor seemed to diminish. His tan even appeared to improve slightly. "Well, that's good news, then. Melanie? Good news, right?"

She could only nod. Unable to cry earlier, she was now making a monumental effort to hold back tears of relief.

His Honor consulted his watch, then fiddled with his French cuffs and gold cuff links. "I'll just have a few words with the press, and then I'll get back to city hall. Can I give you a lift, Melanie?"

"No, thanks, Sam. I'm going to stick around here a little while."

"All right. I'll talk to you soon." He planted a warm kiss on the top of her head, nodded to Mike, then turned and strode toward the waiting reporters.

Melanie glanced at the small stick-figure placard behind Mike that indicated the gender of the rest room. "I'm going in," she said.

"Maybe you better wait, Melanie. I don't know if..."

"I'm going in, Mike." Her hand was already flattened on the door, pushing in.

"Sonny?"

He heard her voice—sweet and soft and full of warmth—just on the other side of the metal door of the stall where he'd been both hiding out and retching for the past fifteen minutes.

He'd witnessed his share of brutal deaths, maybe more than his share of gore and grisliness in fourteen years on the job, but the sight of young Timothy Moore's charred body sitting behind the melted steering wheel of the Corvette had rocked Sonny to his very core. That bomb had been meant for him. That should have been his body, burned beyond recognition. Jesus. Poor Moore.

Well, hell. He could breathe more easily now, knowing Melanie was safe. But she was the last person on earth he wanted to see him right now in this kind of shape, and at the same time she was the only person on earth he desperately needed to see and to hold.

"I'll be right out, babe."

Snagging some john paper, Sonny rubbed the tears from his eyes and the sweat from his face and neck. He pitched the paper into the water, kicked the flush handle with his foot, then turned to slide the bolt on the door.

Melanie was leaning against the bank of sinks. If Sonny had expected her to appear flustered or uncomfortable with being in a men's room, he quickly discovered how wrong he was. His ex-wife stood there like a pillar of calm and confidence. She looked absolutely beautiful and quite serene, except for the fact that her lips trembled slightly when she asked, "Are you okay, sweetheart?"

Now he was. Sonny cleared his throat. "Yeah. I'm fine. Just a little queasy."

He turned the water on in one of the sinks, then cupped his hands under the tap for a couple mouthfuls of cold, clean liquid to swish and spit out. When he finished, Melanie was beside him, handing him a paper towel.

"Thanks." He wiped his face, then dried his hands.

Just as he was about to pull Melanie into his arms, she moved there of her own accord.

"I'm so sorry about Moore," she whispered against his chest. "But so so happy about you."

He tilted his head, pressing his cheek to the fragrant warmth of her hair. "God, that poor kid, Mel." His voice wasn't as steady as he wanted it to be. "It should have been me. Not him."

"It shouldn't have been anybody, love." Her arms tightened around his waist. "It wasn't your fault."

"I guess not... I don't know. Hell."

Sonny's throat clogged and his mouth twisted. He couldn't even speak anymore. All he could do was stand there, feeling Mel's warmth, feeling so damned guilty that he was alive, feeling so goddamned grateful it was Moore instead of him.

"I love you so much, Melanie," he said. "I need you. God, honey, I need you. I'll do whatever you want about a baby. Just let me be with you. Always."

"Always, Sonny. All I want is you. That's all. This morning, when I thought you might be dead..." Her cool composure came apart. "All I want is you. The baby doesn't matter. Not really. Whatever happens, happens. All I want is you."

They stood there a long time, holding each other, holding on for dear life.

Chapter 14

Melanie peeked around the red sandstone brick wall that enclosed the back porch of Sonny's house. She'd been ordered to stay in this protected place a safe distance from the driveway where Sonny and Mike and the guy with the bomb-sniffing German shepherd went over both the minivan and the Miata with mirrors, noses, and the proverbial fine-toothed comb.

She'd also been ordered to pack an overnight bag and informed she wouldn't be coming back to Channing Square until Slink Kinnison was safely behind bars. Ever since they'd emerged from the men's room at the precinct, it seemed all Sonny had done was give her orders. Stay behind him. Keep her head down. Pack. Sit. Stay.

''I don't want to stay at Mike and Connie's. I want

to stay with you," she called out from her little bunker. "Sonny? Did you hear me?"

"I heard you," he called back from the driveway.

Well, hearing her wasn't the same as agreeing with her, was it?

It wasn't that she minded going to Mike and Connie's so much. She just didn't want to leave Sonny. Not now, for heaven's sake. Not when they'd just truly realized how much they loved and needed each other. It was all Melanie could do to remain a hundred feet away from him right now while he checked out the vehicles.

This morning she'd thought she'd lost him forever. She never wanted to feel that way again in her life.

"How much longer?" she called.

"We're almost done."

She sighed, pulled her planner from her handbag, and slid the little pen from its leather loop. So much had changed in the past week that she didn't even know where to begin making lists. After she printed To Do at the top of the page, she just sat there, staring, tapping the pen against her teeth.

They'd have to get married again, obviously, and that meant a blood test, a license, all the details of the ceremony. Did they want a church this time instead of city hall? What about a honeymoon? That would be nice. Mmm. That would be wonderful. But where? And when? How long?

Between them, they owned two houses. Something would have to be done about that. Sell one? Rent one? Get rid of his and hers to find the perfect ours?

Every idea that came into her head seemed to beget another idea, then another. Every problem led to half a dozen more. Every question had myriad possible answers. After several minutes Melanie found herself merely doodling on the margins of the page, making dollar signs and daisy chains and figure eights rather than a neat, numbered, logical list. It wasn't that she couldn't think. And it wasn't because she had once again come under the influence of Chaos, Incorporated. It was just... Well...

It was because she didn't care!

All of a sudden it occurred to her that Sonny didn't disrupt her neat and precise little world. He merely changed its focus. The details that mattered so much when she wasn't with him became insignificant when he was part of her life. All that was important was Sonny.

God, how she loved him!

She closed her planner, then dropped it back in her bag without even bothering to replace the pen in its loop.

"All clear." His sexy, sandpapery voice sounded just above her head and his open hand appeared to help her up.

When she stood, he gazed down at her for a long moment. There was still a trace of red in his beautiful blue eyes, a worried turn to his mouth.

"Mike's going to drive the Miata," he said. "We'll keep it at his place till this all blows over. You, too, Mel. I want you to stay there until I tell you otherwise. No arguing on this one. Kinnison's liable to do anything now.''

"How long do you think it will take until he's brought in?" she asked.

"Not long."

There was something so hard and unyielding in his tone that Melanie knew instantly what Sonny planned to do. This had turned personal for him. Personal, as well as lethal. He blamed himself for Timothy Moore's death, and so Sonny was going after Slink Kinnison on his own, without department approval, without backup, and probably without mercy.

She sucked in a long, slow breath, girding herself to face the inevitable.

"You're risking your job, you know," she said in a meager effort to dissuade him. "If you'd just wait until next week…"

He shook his head. "That'll be too late. I have to do this, Mel. Nobody else in the department can get to him as fast as I can."

"I know." She kissed his chin. "Just be careful, will you?"

"Always, darlin'."

"Okay. I guess we better not keep Mike waiting. I'm ready."

Sonny reached down for her bag. "Hey, it's light," he said, sounding surprised. "Where's that kitchen sink you always pack?"

"I left it in the kitchen for a change," she said, trying to sound far more cheerful than she felt.

"No kidding? You left it? No sewing kit? No seven

pairs of shoes? No umbrella and overshoes just in case?'' He unzipped the big canvas bag a few inches and peered inside. "Jeez, Mel, where's your pillow you absolutely, positively, cannot sleep without?''

Melanie couldn't help but laugh. It was true. She'd wrestled with that one. Leaving behind her sewing kit and umbrella had been fairly easy, though. Leaving behind her pillow that she absolutely, positively, could not sleep without had been nearly impossible. But she'd done it, by God, to prove something to herself as well as to Sonny.

"That was the old me," she said. "You're not the only one who's capable of change, you know, Lieutenant.''

Sonny zipped the bag closed, then looped an arm around her shoulders and grinned. "I believe you. Way to go, Felix. I'm proud of you.''

"Thank you very much.''

He grinned at her for a few more appreciative seconds before he said, "Let's go.''

It was Sonny who was making a mental list now as he backed the minivan out of the driveway, then followed Mike and the Miata down Kassing Avenue and then left onto Channing and past the burned hulk of the Forresters' house.

For all of Slink Kinnison's ability to keep his drug empire intact and below the police radar, the guy was a complete screw-up when it came to exacting revenge. In his attempt to get Sonny to lay off after he'd failed to kill him two weeks ago at the meth lab bust, Slink had had the wrong house torched, and followed that by blowing up the wrong car. By Sonny's calculations, the only thing the idiot had done right so far, God damn him, was kill Lovey.

First on Sonny's list was to make certain Melanie was safely away from Channing Square at the Kaczinski house. He knew Mike couldn't be there all the time, but Connie was a drop-dead shot with the .22 they kept locked in their bedroom closet.

Next on his list was stopping by his loft to change into one of his derelict disguises. He still had two weeks remaining on the lease, and he'd left his undercover wardrobe—greasy, ripped clothes, broken-down shoes, assorted mustaches, beards and theatrical scars—there while he decided whether or not he would wear it again or burn it or pass it on to the next department sucker willing to spend half his life on the streets.

Sonny was done with all that. If he hadn't truly acknowledged that fact before, he did now. He wasn't even all that sure he wanted to be a cop anymore. Not his kind of cop, anyway.

He stole a glance at Melanie's tense face and her clenched hands. "It's going to be fine, Mel," he said. "Don't worry. Once this is over with…"

Before he could finish the sentence, a big blue-and-white and chrome-decked car swerved in front of the minivan, forcing Sonny to turn the wheel abruptly to the right. The van jumped the curb and barely missed slamming into a parking meter. Sonny stomped on the brakes, then rammed the gearshift into Park. Meanwhile, the blue-and-white vehicle had screeched to a stop just a few yards ahead.

Sonny didn't even have to read the rear license plate to know who was behind the wheel. The Big Man. Elijah Biggs.

"What's going on?" Melanie's voice was shaky as she eased her death grip on the dashboard.

"Wait here," he told her. "Lock up after I get out."

"But…"

"Just do it."

Once out of the van, he slammed the door and made sure it was locked before he charged toward the blue-and-white pimp mobile parked just ahead at a hazardous angle. Out of the corner of his eye he was aware that Mike had circled around in the Miata and was waiting to cut across the center line to join him. He offered a silent little prayer of thanks for a partner who religiously checked his rearview mirror.

Elijah Biggs was attempting to heave his four-hundred-pound bulk out of his car. The sun flashed on his diamond rings and gold necklaces and turned the chrome on his vehicle a blinding silver. Something else caught Sonny's attention. The sunlight glittering off a chrome-plated pistol in the pimp's big fist.

He reached for his own weapon while he crouched behind the car's trunk and shouted, "Put the gun down, Biggs."

The huge man, only half out from behind the wheel, bellowed something Sonny couldn't understand.

"I said drop it, Elijah. Put the gun down. Now."

Mike was suddenly at Sonny's shoulder, breathing hard, his weapon drawn. "What the hell's going on?"

Keeping an eye on the big man with the big chrome gun, Sonny replied, "Beats me." He shouted to the pimp again. "Put the gun down and let's talk, Elijah."

"We can talk after I kill that son of a bitch who murdered my little Lovey," Biggs wailed. His black face was glistening with sweat and his eyes were wild and wet with tears.

Sonny and Mike exchanged quick glances. "What son of a bitch?" Sonny called.

"Slink. That's who. The son of a bitch who killed my Lovey." The pimp had about three hundred pounds angled out of the car now. He was waving his gun while he screamed. "I'm gonna blow the sucker's head off."

"You know where he is?" Mike asked.

"Damned straight I know. He's in there. I just got a call from one of my girls."

Biggs gestured toward the tan brick building to the right of his car. Until that moment, Sonny hadn't paid much attention to any of the businesses that lined this block of Grant Parkway. He realized now that Elijah had pulled up in front of one of the massage parlors that the city fathers were trying so hard to outlaw.

"What do you think?" he asked Mike.

"I think we better hog-tie Biggs before he hurts somebody."

"Yeah." It was one time in his life Sonny wished

he were a civilian and didn't have to be concerned
with public safety. He muttered an oath. "I don't suppose we can just wait for them to kill each other, can
we?"

The huge pimp had finally extracted himself from
his vehicle and was now pointing his gun across the
hood of his car at the massage parlor's painted-over-
plate-glass window. Before Sonny or Mike could call
out to stop him, he fired. The sound of shattering glass
was barely audible over the man's shouts.

"Get your ass out here, Slink. You hear me? You
killed my Lovey. Now I'm gonna kill you."

"Go around and cover the back door," Sonny told
Mike. As he spoke he glanced over his shoulder toward the minivan to make sure Melanie wasn't sitting
there making herself a target. He didn't see her, which
meant she had ducked down onto the seat or better
yet the floor. He hoped.

"Not a chance, partner. I'm staying right here to
make sure you don't do something stupid," Mike
said. "If Kinnison goes out the back, we'll get him
later."

"I don't want him later, goddammit. I want him
now."

Elijah Biggs fired another round into the premises,
shattering what little glass remained within the window frame.

"Hey! There are women in there, Biggs," Sonny
yelled. "Put the weapon away and let us take care of
Slink."

"I'm gonna take care of the sucker right between his eyes, the way he deserves."

Sirens began wailing in the distance. Somebody inside must have called 9-1-1. Hell, it was probably Slink himself who'd called, figuring the only way he'd get out alive would be through police intervention.

Biggs fired again, but this time there was return fire from inside the massage parlor. Bullets from a semiautomatic rifle dinged into the pimp mobile and zinged over Sonny's and Mike's heads as they ducked further down, caught in the crossfire.

"We gotta get out of here," Mike said. There was a note of panic in his voice. "We're sitting ducks if..."

Slink Kinnison came crashing out the door, firing wildly.

With Biggs on one side and the madman with the semiautomatic on the other, Sonny and Mike had no choice but to nearly flatten themselves on the sidewalk. Sonny couldn't even get off a decent shot underneath the car to take Slink out at the knees.

"Don't do anything stupid, Son," Mike growled at him.

"Don't worry."

It occurred to him all of a sudden that Mike had ample reason to worry. If this had happened a couple of weeks ago, Sonny probably wouldn't have been able to resist taking both shooters down with a full frontal assault. He didn't know if it was the rush of adrenaline he couldn't resist or some misguided instinct to play the hero.

But whatever it was, it was gone. All he wanted to do was to get out of this in one piece and get on with his life with Melanie.

Bullets were everywhere now, direct hits thunking into metal and ricochets zinging off the pavement. He glanced over his shoulder again to make sure Mel was keeping her pretty head down. When he saw a couple bullet holes in the van's grill, he decided it was time to put an end to this. Somehow.

Biggs couldn't have too many rounds left in his clip, but Sonny didn't want to get hit by the one he hadn't counted on.

"I'm gonna crawl under the car, Mikey, and see if I can't get a clean shot at Kinnison."

"Okay. Go."

Sonny began to elbow his way under the rear bumper and exhaust system. He didn't even want to think about a stray bullet igniting the gas tank. He was all the way under the car, inching forward, when he heard Mike scream, "Jeez! I'm hit."

For a second Sonny didn't know whether to go forward or to scramble back. Just then Slink Kinnison strafed the pavement beside the pimp mobile, forcing Sonny to cover his head with his arms to avoid the bits of concrete spraying all around him.

When the sharp hail subsided, he lifted his head an inch just in time to see Kinnison's right knee touch the pavement. Had he been hit? After a second of blessed relief, Sonny realized just how wrong he was.

The drug dealer hadn't been hit. His left knee came down, followed by his chest and shoulders, and finally his ugly, smirking face framed by greasy yellow hair. The guy hadn't been hit at all. He was kneeling, and now he was holding the semiautomatic a few inches off the sidewalk, aiming directly under the car.

Dammit to hell. Why wasn't Biggs shooting anymore? Somewhere Sonny could hear squealing tires and the roar of an engine, but he knew the squad car pulling up had arrived too late for him as he stared into Slink Kinnison's twisted face and the black barrel of his rifle.

Sonny aimed his gun ahead of him, knowing the best he could do from his awkward angle under the belly of the low-slung car would be to hit a toe, a foot, maybe an ankle if he was lucky. He hoped he wasn't dead before he knew where the bullet struck.

He squinted and squeezed off a shot, knowing it would probably be the last thing he would ever do. Except think about Mel. Think hard about Mel. God. Mel.

Then—what the hell?—he couldn't see a thing, and it took several seconds for Sonny to realize that his view of Slink and the AK-47 and imminent death had been obstructed by the sudden appearance of a tire. A portion of a tire from his vantage point, and a semicircle of hubcap that looked vaguely familiar.

He blinked away his confusion. My God. It was the minivan.

Melanie couldn't stop shaking. She could hardly breathe.

"Melanie, open the door!"

She tried but she couldn't unwrap her fingers from the steering wheel.

"Honey, open the door! Open the window!"

Her mouth tasted funny. Terrible. Like copper. Some bitter metal. Some dry metallic filings that she tried to swallow but couldn't.

"Somebody get a slim jim. Now. I need to pop this goddamn door. Melanie! Melanie!"

She tried to swallow again. She thought if she swallowed, the coppery taste would go away and then she'd be able to think about something else.

"Come on. Come on. The engine's running and the damn van's still in gear. My wife's in shock. I need to get her out of there."

Sonny? She turned her head to the left, encountering those familiar, beautiful blue-green eyes. He was alive!

She swallowed. Hard. The coppery taste disappeared.

Five hours later it was just getting dark outside and the shift was changing at the precinct when word finally came that the DA's office wouldn't be filing charges against Melanie. Slink Kinnison's death, when she'd hit him with the minivan, had been ruled a justifiable homicide.

"They should give you a medal," Sam Venneman said, draining the last of his coffee from a foam cup. "In fact, that's not such a bad idea." His lips quirked in a grin. "I might mention it at my next press conference."

"I don't want a medal, Sam. Please. I just want to go home." Melanie reached across the battered table to pat his hand, glad that her own hands weren't shaking anymore. "Thank you for all your help."

He shrugged his fashionably padded, pin-striped shoulders. "Can I give you a lift?"

Melanie shook her head. "I'll wait for Sonny. He should be back from the hospital any minute."

After Sam left, she stared at the big, round institutional clock on the wall, watching the second hand make its repeated sweeps and listening to muted conversations out in the corridor. She didn't feel like a murderer. Mostly she felt numb. She hadn't meant to kill Slink Kinnison, only to keep him from killing Sonny. Apparently, from what the EMTs had said, the drug dealer's head hit the pavement and he died instantly.

She wasn't sharing in the joy that was going around the precinct as a result, but she didn't think she'd be having nightmares about it the rest of her life or even need the services of a shrink to help her cope. In fact, she'd do it again if she had to, to save her husband's life.

Funny. Sometime during the past few hours she'd stopped thinking of Sonny as her ex.

The door to the interrogation room opened and there he was as if her thoughts had somehow conjured him up. He looked tired. She couldn't wait to get him home and tucked into bed.

"How's Mike?" Melanie asked.

"He's out of surgery. His knee's pretty torn up, but he'll be fine."

"That's good." She sighed and stood. "Can we go home now?"

"Absolutely." Sonny looped an arm around her. "Let's get out of here. We've got a future to plan, Felix, you and I. We've got lists to write."

Melanie smiled and rested her head against his strong shoulder. "And love to make."

"That, too, baby," he said softly. "That, too."

Epilogue

Christmas Eve the following year

Melanie was hanging the last of her father's stained-glass ornaments on the tree just as she heard Sonny's footsteps coming down the stairs.

"Is she asleep?" she asked.

"Out like a little light. I had to sing sixteen choruses of 'Rudolph the Red-Nosed Reindeer,' though."

"Sixteen?" Melanie laughed. "You actually counted?"

"Pretty sick, isn't it? You must be rubbing off on me, Felix." He picked a glass ornament out of the box. "Where do you want this one?"

"Anyplace," she said, taking a few steps back and surveying the tree. "Well, maybe on the right. We could use a few more over there."

"Here?"

"Lower."

"Here?"

"Maybe two inches up and to the right. Okay. Now up about half an inch. Stop. Right there."

Sonny shook his head. "Mel, you're the only person I know who says 'anyplace' and means anyplace within a millimeter of exactly where you want it."

"Uh-huh," she said in total agreement. "Now we need another ornament about two inches above that one."

While she stood watching and offering advice, Melanie was also debating when to tell Sonny she was pregnant again. It would make for a lovely Christmas Eve, but then again the news would be a wonderful gift tomorrow morning.

This was so much better than the holiday she'd originally planned when she'd decided to have a baby. Back then, she had pictured herself alone with a just-beginning-to-walk Alex or Alexis. Now she had Sonny and a just-beginning-to-walk Sadie whose blue-green eyes were the image of her daddy's and whose stubborn notions of order included oatmeal everywhere but in her mouth and toys every place but her toybox. The Princess of Pandemonium.

Melanie had never been happier.

Sonny had turned in his badge and his service weapon when Mike and his bum knee went on disability, and the two of them had formed a partnership, rehabbing first Sonny's house and then others in Channing Square. Both men looked far better, far sex-

ier in tool belts than they ever had in shoulder hol-
sters. Of course, they'd both looked divine in their
dark blue suits at city hall when she and Sonny re-
married.

Sadie arrived nine months to the day—Melanie
counted, of course—after their fierce lovemaking in
the shower. Their next child was due on the Fourth
of July.

Maybe by that time she'd have a better handle on
motherhood, Melanie hoped. For someone so thoroughly organized and in control, she still tended to
fly apart at fevers above a hundred and tears that
lasted longer than ten minutes.

It was Sonny who took to parenting as if he'd been
born to do just that. She doubted he'd want to stop
at two.

"To the left about an inch," she said.

"Here?"

"One branch higher."

"Here?"

"Perfect," she said.

Everything was. Perfect. Almost as if she'd planned
it.

* * * * *

▼™ SILHOUETTE®
SENSATION™

AVAILABLE FROM 18TH OCTOBER 2002

CAPTURING CLEO Linda Winstead Jones

he enemies of sultry Cleo Tanner were being murdered—but why? Detective
uther Malone decided to find out by getting close to her. Would he catch the
ller or just find himself captured by Cleo?

HOT AS ICE Merline Lovelace

ode Name: Danger

rozen in the Arctic for forty-five years, Major Charles Stone was woken—by
eautiful Dr Diana Remington. Diana welcomed his heated touch—but
meone seemed determined to let sleeping spies lie—forever…

RETURN OF THE PRODIGAL SON Ruth Langan

he Lassiter Law

eautiful widow and mother Andi Brady needed Donovan Lassiter's help to
ove her late husband's innocence. But ex CIA agent Donovan found himself in
anger—of losing his heart…

BORN IN SECRET Kylie Brant

irst-Born Sons

xy spy Walker James was incensed to learn that former flame Jasmine LeBarr
as his partner on his new mission. Could they safeguard the kingdom and
kindle their passionate past?

THE RENEGADE STEALS A LADY Vickie Taylor

arco Angelosi would risk *everything* to protect former lover Paige Burkett—
'd even go to prison for a crime he hadn't committed. Paige had to convince
m that love isn't about making sacrifices…but holding on.

PROMISES, PROMISES Shelley Cooper

retchen Montgomery had promised a dying friend that she would have a wild,
azy affair—but once she'd done it, she found out she was pregnant! Would the
ther, confirmed bachelor Dr Marco Garibaldi, propose?

DELIVERED BY
Christmas

Linda Howard
Joan Hohl   Sandra Steffen

Available from 18th October 2002

Available at most branches of WH Smith,
Tesco, Martins, Borders, Eason, Sainsbury's
and all good paperback bookshops.

1102/128/SH41

2 FREE

books and a surprise gift!

We would like to take this opportunity to thank you for reading this Silhouette® book by offering you the chance to take TWO more specially selected titles from the Sensation™ series absolutely FREE! We're also making this offer to introduce you to the benefits of the Reader Service™—

- ★ FREE home delivery
- ★ FREE gifts and competitions
- ★ FREE monthly Newsletter
- ★ Exclusive Reader Service discount
- ★ Books available before they're in the shops

Accepting these FREE books and gift places you under no obligation to buy, you may cancel at any time, even after receiving your free shipment. Simply complete your details below and return the entire page to the address below. *You don't even need a stamp!*

YES! Please send me 2 free Sensation books and a surprise gift. I understand that unless you hear from me, I will receive 4 superb new titles every month for just £2.85 each, postage and packing free. I am under no obligation to purchase any books and may cancel my subscription at any time. The free books and gift will be mine to keep in any case.

S2ZEA

Ms/Mrs/Miss/Mr ....Initials..................................
BLOCK CAPITALS PLEASE

Surname ....

Address ....

....

....Postcode ....

Send this whole page to:
UK: FREEPOST CN81, Croydon, CR9 3WZ
EIRE: PO Box 4546, Kilcock, County Kildare (stamp required)